A SUGAR CREEK CHRISTMAS

A SUGAR CREEK NOVEL

JENNY B. JONES

SWEET PEA PRODUCTIONS

For information contact:
Jen@jennybjones.com

FREE EBOOK OFFER

Sign up for my newsletter and be the first to know about my new releases, book discounts, and giveaways.
As a bonus, receive a **FREE** ebook!
www.jennybjones.com/news

Dedicated to Judy Wilkerson

Thank you for laughs, vacation fun, barn cats, shopping, peach pie,
and my compulsion to return eighty-percent of what I buy.
You'll always be my favorite aunt.

1

"Emma, you're fired."

Three days after Thanksgiving, Emma Sutton sat in the executive offices of America's favorite morning news program.

"I don't think I heard you correctly, Mr. Peterson." She tilted her head to her other ear because surely she had not heard correctly. Not that she had a bad ear. But at thirty, perhaps she was entering that phase where things started falling apart. Like her auditory abilities. "Because it sounded like you said—"

"I'm firing you."

"But news anchors make on-air gaffes all the time. Yesterday's blunder was a grave mistake, but it was just that—a mistake. Yesterday's error, tomorrow's YouTube gold, right?" A bead of sweat tracked down her chest beneath her tailored blazer. It was miserably hot in this office. A bit of air and some water would've been nice. And the ability to click her heels and do yesterday all over.

"You told America you hated Christmas."

"I did do that, sir. But I've apologized a hundred times."

"You said you *hated* Christmas." Her boss repeated the statement slowly, as if Emma hadn't gotten it the first time. As if she didn't understand the enormity of her holiday-bashing remark.

"If I may speak freely—"

"I don't recommend it," he drawled. "I've had so many phone calls in protest of your on-air declaration, it briefly shut down our system. And that's just from the local affiliates. Then there are the emails from viewers and a virtual hate storm on social media." Mr. Peterson rested his elbows on his dark oak desk and laced his fingers. The eyes looking at Emma over rimless glasses did not hold their usual paternal kindness.

The darn tears clouded Emma's vision yet again, and she worried she would soon lose her ability to speak without choking on a blubbering sob. Last night she had sat with her laptop in bed and read thousands upon thousands of hateful sentiments online, viewers demanding Emma's job. She'd been too upset to answer phone calls from her family and friends. She hadn't even been able to choke down two bites of Chunky Monkey. The Chunk was always there for her.

"Sir, I think if you'd let me resume my duties as soon as possible and let me apologize to our viewers, it could begin the mending process. We have such loyal fans. They're not going to be okay with Tevyn in my place." That little twerp had wanted her job forever. Tevyn, of the cutesie name, Victoria's Secret model face, and a voice any female broadcast journalist would commit petty crimes to have. She filled in when Emma was on assignment, and the twiggy waif had been gunning for Emma's seat as a regular on the *Sunrise News* couch.

"I've been part of the show's family for three years,"

Emma said. "I'm one of the team. Who will read the entertainment report? The Royals went to Australia yesterday. Nobody can report that like me. Does Tevyn have contacts in Buckingham palace like I do? Does she have any idea whose dress a certain princess wore yesterday? There's a major impending Hollywood divorce brewing and—"

"Emma, you've left me with no choice."

"But I'm on the fast track here; we both know this. You said I might be co-anchoring within five years. I'm ready to do that. I'm ready to cut my hair into a sensible bob, brush up on my foreign policy, and be that star for you. Just let me look right into that camera, admit my mistake, and beg forgiveness."

"It's not that easy. With all this global unrest, this country can count on the beauty of only a few things, and one of them is Christmas."

"The biggest retail event of the year?"

Mr. Peterson's hand slammed on his legal pad. "The season of love! Tidings of great joy!"

Emma blinked and tried not to shrink further into her seat. "Right. I knew that. Yes, Christmas is awesome. Peace on earth, good will to man. All of that. Indeed."

His eyes narrowed as he studied her. "What you may or may not believe about the holiday season is not the issue. Our viewers do not want to hear their morning sweetheart tell them"—he held his notebook at arm's length and peered through his glasses— "Christmas is stupid and promoted by a society of naive lemmings."

"It does sound bad."

"Bad? Bad is Tanner's bout of hiccups during the severe weather coverage last month. What I saw yesterday was a television personality drop an atomic bomb on her career *and* our network."

Emma shifted uncomfortably. "Might I mention my mic should not have been on?"

"Is that really where you'd like me to put the blame?"

"No." She knew the rule. Always assume the mic was on. Always.

Her career was in the proverbial toilet, swirling furiously around the bowl, ready to be sucked away and spewed into the sewer. "I'll do whatever it takes to redeem this."

Mr. Peterson pinched the bridge of his nose, closed his eyes, and inhaled deeply. "Emma, I have to wonder if you truly do want to redeem this."

"What? Of course I do." Visions of eating Ramen soup and living out of her car danced in her head. "I need this job."

"Lately your work has lost its luster."

"My piece on celebrities' favorite candy might've been a little lacking."

"You've been at this since college. It's normal to experience burnout and—"

"I'm *fine*. Maybe I'm just ready for a new challenge." Yes, that was it. A new challenge would breathe life into her career. She had to admit, she was bored. There was more to her abilities than reporting on celebrity gossip and the latest heart-warming dog video.

"Well, I'm about to give you a new challenge. You're still fired."

Her hazel eyes burned with unshed tears. "I was thinking more along the lines of sending me to D.C. to report on politics. Or a war zone." *Pretty much the same thing.*

Mr. Peterson leaned back in his seat taking his first relaxed posture of the meeting. He crossed his arms over his sweater-covered chest. "Officially, we'll tell everyone you're taking a sabbatical."

She sniffed and swallowed past the emotional clog in her throat. "And when I don't return?"

"Maybe you do return."

"I. . . I don't understand."

"Here's the deal. You've done lethal damage here. The only thing that can restore this disaster is for you to go away. Let the viewers forget you for a bit."

"Last week they loved me."

"There's currently an online campaign to surrender you to the Mother's Christmas League of Dallas to stick you on top of their twenty-foot Alpine spruce."

"That's a bit harsh."

"It has seven thousand signatures."

Emma yanked a tissue from her purse and blotted her eyes.

Mr. Peterson's voice softened to that familiar tone that had supported and encouraged her during her time at the network. "To save your image, it will require a lot more than just disappearing for a while. I've got to save our show, but as for saving your career, that's going to be a bit more difficult. Are you willing to do what it takes?"

All she could do was nod.

"Your little vacation runs until the new year. But by Christmas, I want you to bring me the most beautiful, inspirational story you can find, something so moving, no reader will be left unaffected."

"Where am I going to get this story?"

"That's up to you. You're a reporter. Use your journalistic nose. But if I don't have a fully-developed human interest piece by December twenty-fifth, one that no other station has a hint of, something that makes our readers weep with joy, restores their faith in humanity *and* in you, then your sabbatical becomes a termination."

"But I don't know where to even look for—"

"Your correct response here is *thank you.*"

She straightened. "Yes, sir. Thank you, Mr. Peterson."

Her boss eased off his glasses and regarded his fallen news star. "I don't know what happened that makes you dislike Christmas. But it's about to cause you to lose a career you've worked your tail off for. Turn this around—for the network and for yourself."

Emma stood and gathered her purse, the memories pelting her like sleet. "I can do this."

"Find Christmas, Emma," Mr. Peterson's voice boomed like a heralding angel. "Find your Christmas."

2

Two flights, two layovers, and too many airport pretzels later, Emma stood on a familiar front porch in Sugar Creek, Arkansas.

She rapped her knuckles on the door.

After a handful of minutes passed without a response, a slender senior citizen finally appeared. She lifted one judgmental brow then let her blue eyes roam over Emma from her long, brown hair to the toes of her red flats. "I just called in my Avon order, I don't need my yard mowed, and yes, I know Jesus."

Emma's lips quirked. "Because you were in the same graduating class?"

The woman threw back her blonde head and laughed. "I hope you've got a kiss for your grandma with that sassy mouth."

Emma dropped a bag and smiled. "Hello, Granny Dearest."

Sylvie let her granddaughter cross the threshold into the house, then pulled her into a tight embrace. "Welcome home, sugar."

Emma allowed the familiar scent of her grandmother and her beloved home to wash over her. If comfort had a fragrance, it was Sylvie. "I have royally screwed up," Emma mumbled against the woman's shoulder.

"There's a first time for everything." Sylvie patted her granddaughter's back then stepped away to get another good look at her. "Welcome to life on the not-so-perfect side." She winked. "We drink a lot here."

Emma craned her neck at the sound of laughter down the hall. "Am I interrupting something?"

"Sexy Book Club. Come join us."

"*What* kind of club?" Just the thought of making small talk with Sylvie's collection of friends made Emma want to cry with the weight of exhaustion.

"Sexy Book Club. We read steamy romance novels, throw back cocktails, and eat cookies. There's a four-page wait list to get in our group."

"Someone can have my spot tonight. I'll just slip on up to my room."

"The girls have been expecting you. Two of your cousins even made it." With a manicured hand, Sylvie brushed a strand of hair from Emma's cheek, just like she'd done a million times when Emma had been a little girl. "Take your bags upstairs, wipe the mascara tracks off your face, then pop in just for a few minutes. You're my famous granddaughter. I want to show you off."

"You could just show them the YouTube clips instead."

"I meant famous for your hard work and brilliant journalism."

"Are you sure your idea is going to work?" Not that Emma had any others.

"This town is turning into a Christmas mecca. You're in just the right place for some inspiration, holiday spirit, and whatever other bunk your TV show needs. I've got it all arranged."

Emma exhaled weakly, too tired to even take a good, deep breath. "You better have a big platter of your sugar cookies waiting."

"Had to hide them from Frannie, but I saved them. Can you hear them calling your name?"

"Pretty sure that's my bed I hear."

Sylvie gave her a swat on the rear. "Get to stepping. I'll buy you some time before the hen brigade descends on you."

Emma picked up her giant bag and made it as far as the first step before her grandmother's voice stopped her.

"Em?"

"Yes?"

"I'm glad you're home."

Home.

The word sounded like poetry, like decadence.

"Thanks, Sylvie. But I'm just visiting." Emma turned back to the staircase and made her way to the top.

A home was something Emma had never had.

And probably never would.

"THERE SHE IS!"

As soon as Emma stepped into the den, her slender frame was swallowed up in a group hug that felt more like a linebacker's tackle. In a matter of seconds she was the center of a huddle that consisted of a few of her cousins, Sylvie's best friend, and three women Emma had never laid eyes on.

"Losing oxygen here," she mumbled into someone's neck.

"I've missed you!" said Hattie, one of her cousins.

"Missed her more!" from a voice that could've been Hattie's sister.

"Didn't you eat in that big city?"

"You got a boyfriend?"

"Hey!" Emma ducked out of the swarm. "Someone was getting a little too handsy."

Her grandmother sniffed. "Just seeing if the boobies were still real."

I should've followed my instinct to lock myself in my room and sleep. "It's all real." The boobs, being fired from her dream job, being ticked at a stinking holiday. *Real.*

"Come on in. Sit down." Hattie reached for Emma's hand and led her to one of the leather couches. A warm fire crackled and danced in the fireplace. Though it was only late November, the Northwest corner of Arkansas often jumped right from fall to winter with little transition, like an impatient, hyper child.

Due to the demands of her job, Emma hadn't been back to Sugar Creek in over five years. She had worked nearly every holiday since leaving college, desperate to pull ahead of the competition and climb to top billing of a network news show fast. It had been within her reach, too.

Until I opened my big mouth.

"So what are you guys reading?" Emma accepted a plate of finger foods from Sylvie and mentally recalled a list of titles recently discussed at the water cooler and on the show.

"*The Hot Sheik's Pregnant Secretary*."

Emma choked on a chocolate chip.

Hattie handed her a drink. "We tried to go with picks from the newspaper, but they bored us."

"I've learned a lot." Frannie Nelson wagged her brows. "If you know what I mean." Frannie and Sylvie were like mac and cheese, peanut butter and jelly. They'd worked together for years, retired at the same time, and were both widowed and on the hunt. While Sylvie was fair-skinned and blonde, Frannie had a beautiful mahogany complexion and had let some of her muscle ease into curves.

"My counselor told me I needed a more constructive hobby than my daily target practice," Sylvie said.

Emma's grandmother had raised her since Emma was fourteen. Sylvie had worked as a top-level, top-secret *something* in the CIA, as had Frannie. What the women did was still vague, classified, and possibly a little exaggerated. Part-time work had been Sylvie's choice while Emma was in her custody, but as soon as Emma went to college, Sylvie had returned to her double life. Her grandmother and Frannie had only retired in the last year, and Emma wasn't convinced the two were completely removed from the agency.

Her grandmother ran her painted fingernails through her short hair. "I started the group so Frannie and I could discuss life as a civilian, but that talking about your feelings crap got old after the first meeting. So we moved on to something else." Sylvie shrugged. "Turns out I like books."

"When she's not at the casino," Hattie whispered.

Emma reached for her cousin's dog-eared paperback. "Books about men with no shirts, apparently."

"The shirts would get in the way of their life's work," Frannie said.

"And what work is this?" Emma heard herself ask.

"Firemen, policemen, Navy Seals," Sylvie said with a little too much gusto. "Or just being sexy."

Frannie fanned herself with her copy. "It's a full-time job."

Sylvie patted Emma's hand. "Before we delve into our

first book about an Arabian prince and his lady, I want to make sure everyone knows my granddaughter, Emma."

"Didn't I see you on the internet?" A woman her grandmother's age pulled out her phone and began to do a quick search. "You look so familiar."

"She's a well-known morning television host," Sylvie said. "My Emma's just taking a little break to spend the holiday with her family."

"And we're glad," Hattie said. "Plus it takes the heat off me and my divorce."

Emma knew every tidbit about celebrity gossip, but very little about the latest happenings with her own family. "Glad I could help."

"And gets the book club ladies off my back with their match-making." Hattie took a healthy bite of a cookie. "So Sylvie said something about you doing some work while you're here?"

"I'll be filling in for Melissa Jackson while she's on her maternity leave. Mayor Conway hired me."

The women took a collective pause before exploding into mayhem.

"Oh, no."

"Dear, Lord, somebody tell her."

"This is bad."

"That man screws up *everything!*"

"Wait." Emma held up her hand to silence the swell of chatter. "Tell me what?"

"Shug"—Sylvie popped a bite of cheese between her lips—"Mayor Conway unexpectedly passed away last week."

"I just talked to him a week ago Sunday."

"He died on Monday," Frannie said.

This wasn't part of the plan. *"Come back to Arkansas,"* her grandmother had said. "*I've got the perfect job for you to get your Christmas story.*"

"He promised me Melissa's position," Emma reminded them.

"Even in death that man can't be trusted." Frannie blew out a sigh.

Emma turned to her grandmother, gritting her teeth. "Why didn't you tell me before I paid the neighbor kid to get my mail, locked up my apartment, and drove all the way here?"

"Because, my little pistol, I wanted to see my granddaughter."

The doorbell clanged, and the women in the room stilled.

"Well, who could that be?" Sylvie set her plate on the side table and stood.

"Want me to cover you?" Frannie reached into her jacket.

"No!" Emma turned inspecting eyes back to Sylvie. "There will be no covering anyone tonight. And what is that rhinestone thing sticking out from your sweater?"

"My new holster. It's supposed to be concealing, but clearly I need a refund."

Though the doorbell rang again, Emma ignored it. "You ladies are *retired*. Do you get that you're no longer in the field? And you *are* in Sugar Creek. There are no bad guys here. No terrorists. No dirty politicians."

Frannie harumphed.

"Okay, a few dirty politicians," Emma conceded. "But no drug cartels."

"Because they're afraid of us. We keep this town safe," Sylvie said.

Frannie grinned. "We're legends."

As Sylvie slipped to the foyer, Emma rubbed her left

temple where a headache had begun to pound. There was only one thing that put an ache in that spot. Her family.

All her life, Emma had prayed for a normal family. Her mom, Sylvie's daughter, had been so blissfully traditional. When Elizabeth Casey had unexpectedly died only months after Emma's eighth birthday, the world had gone dark and cold. Emma's father, Edward, had sold their house and many of their belongings, and the two took to the road so he could pursue his burgeoning music career. They lived in motels and apartments, never staying in one place long enough for Emma to make friends.

Until Sylvie stepped in. But Sylvie hadn't exactly been the stereotypical grandmother.

"Your grandmother's retirement from the CIA has not been an easy transition," Frannie said as she bit into another cookie. "For me either."

"It's your third time to retire," Emma said. "No more victory laps."

"We decided this was it," Frannie said. "For real. I like this town, and I'm going to stay. Though it's proving hard to find myself a strong, black man to be my next mister. Lots of white folks here."

Emma smiled at her honorary aunt. "Maybe you need to broaden your horizons."

Frannie smacked her palm against the novel. "That's exactly what these books are teaching me. But I've also yet to find one single sheik."

"So basically," Hattie said, "they've given up international espionage for the romantic kind. You won't be here thirty-six hours before the ladies will be trying to fix you up."

"Girls, look who stopped by." Sylvie reappeared, her arm around a tall, smiling man.

Emma dropped her cookie into her lap and simply stared. The man's eyes lit on her, and his smile disappeared.

"Hello, Emma," Noah Kincaid said. He stood in her grandmother's living room as if he belonged, as if he were comfortable anywhere. Ten years had passed, but his brown eyes still crinkled when he smiled, and his dark hair was still full with that same tendency to fall onto his forehead. He was no longer the skinny college boy, but the very well-proportioned man who didn't appear to be a stranger to the gym.

"Wow, Em." Hattie consulted her watch. "You were here less than an hour."

Noah Kincaid. The boy she had loved in college. The one she'd said yes to when he'd gone down on one knee and proposed her junior year. And the one whose heart she'd stomped on when she'd broken it off, leaving him with nothing more than a letter and her ink-smudged regrets.

"Hello, Noah," Emma managed. "It's been a while."

"Small world, huh?" Sylvie's twinkling eyes darted from Noah to Emma. "I never dreamed Noah would stop by."

"You stopped by the office yesterday and told me to drop in," he said evenly. "A leaky faucet?"

"Yes." Sylvie bobbed her head a little too enthusiastically. "It's in the guest bathroom upstairs. But sit down for a spell. We were just starting our book discussion."

Settling in for a visit looked like the last thing Noah wanted to do. He rubbed the back of his neck, just like he used to do so many years ago, a tell-tale sign he was upset or very uncomfortable. Like when sitting in a living room full of women that included his ex-fiancée.

"What are you ladies reading?"

Frannie piped up first. "*The Hot Sheik's Pregnant*—"

"*War and Peace*!" Sylvie said quickly. "Woo! What a page-turner that one's been, eh, ladies?"

"Yes." Emma finally found her voice again. "Why don't you give us a quick summary?"

"We don't want to bore dear Noah with that." Sylvie shot Emma a warning glare. "The mayor here has better things to do."

Emma frowned. "Mayor?"

"Oh." Sylvie clutched the pearls at her throat. "I was going to tell you. After Mayor Conway kicked the bucket, Noah here was voted in for the interim. Isn't that the most delightful news? I mean, not that the mayor keeled over, but that Sugar Creek is now under Noah's fine leadership."

Emma thought she might throw up her cookie. "I thought I would be working for Mayor Conway. I came all the way to Sugar Creek to take his marketing director's maternity leave."

"I'm sure your job is secure." Sylvie handed Noah a plate. "My Emma has always been a whiz of an event planner. If anyone can continue Melissa's work organizing our town events, it's her. Right, Frannie?"

Frannie sipped something that smelled a little strong to be just fruit punch. "I'd trust Emma to organize a government coup."

"That's very"—Noah's voice was dry as a barren twig—"reassuring."

"Oh, before you take a look at my sink, I made your favorite—a chocolate pie." Sylvie dashed from the room, and the women immediately filled the silence with small talk for the new mayor.

Noah was the mayor? What in the world? The two had met in high school in Sugar Creek and gone to the same college in Oklahoma. Being the only two from the small town in Arkansas, they'd gone from acquaintances to friends to. . . an engaged couple. Emma knew Noah had moved back home after securing his bachelor's degree and had gone to law school at the University of Arkansas. He'd always had big dreams of opening his own practice. But now he would be her boss?

"Here we go!" Sylvie breezed back to the living room, holding a pie like it was an offering of gold. And maybe it was. The woman might not have been the most domestic thing, but she could always bake. "Homemade graham cracker crust, a little surprise layer of ganache, and meringue that is peaked and toasted to perfection."

Frannie tipped back her cup. "The hot sheik would approve."

"Thank you, Sylvie." Noah said.

"You betcha, hon." Sylvie's smile was too sweet, too grandmotherly. "Wanted to give this to you before I put you to work."

"You didn't have to do that," Noah said. "You know you can call me for help any time."

"I know, baby. Because you're always so nice. When I need a hand, who do I call, Frannie?"

Frannie raised her cup. "Noah!"

"And when you had that raccoon in your garage, who did you call?"

"The man who used to make my explosives."

"No, after that."

"Noah!"

"Emma, he's just going to make the best mayor ever," Sylvie said. "He's been on the planning commission for years, and you would not believe all the changes. Tomorrow morning you're going to see a whole new Sugar Creek. And wait till you get a load of all the holiday plans." She handed

Noah his pie. "And Noah, my Emma will be at city hall first thing in the morning to start her new job."

Ah, there it was. Sylvie had anticipated his resistance.

"We should probably talk about that." For only the second time that night, Noah's gaze found Emma. "It might be best if I found someone who—"

"Emma will be in your office at nine o'clock." Sylvie was a woman used to getting her way by any means necessary. "I'm so glad she'll be working for someone as wonderful as you. You need the temporary help, and she needs the temporary work. It's just a match made in heaven."

Judging by Noah's face, he did not believe heaven was the source of this situation.

He set his bribery pie on a nearby table. "I'd better see to your sink." He walked by Emma and paused, his eyes lingering, as if adjusting to the sight of the girl he had known—had loved—now ten years older. "Welcome back to Sugar Creek." His smile as he passed held no warmth. "And just in time for your favorite holiday."

She watched him walk away. That was the man who had once held her whole heart.

And thanks to the news story she desperately needed, Noah Kincaid now held her future.

3

"Mr. Kincaid will see you now."

Emma smiled at that the next morning.

Mr. Kincaid. So formal. But Noah was a somebody now. While she . . . . well, who she was right now was a little bit up in the air. She certainly wasn't an attorney/mayor.

Emma stepped inside the office and shoved all her nerves behind her professional mask of confidence and calm.

"Hello, Emma." Noah didn't bother to smile, and he certainly didn't bother to soften his annoyed tone.

She had lain awake most of the night, letting various scenarios of this meeting play in her head until she had flicked on the bedside lamp at four a.m. and read until it was time for breakfast with Sylvie. Her mental role-playing had still not prepared her. He looked as devastatingly attractive as ever, even with that scowl.

"Good morning, Noah." Emma steadied her voice, just like she did when reporting disturbing events on the show. "It's been a long time." And hadn't time been good to him?

"So you're back in town." He gestured to one of the two seats in front of his desk.

Emma settled into one and crossed her legs, wishing she could rub her sweaty palms on her skirt. "Yes, temporarily. The mayor and I had discussed my starting these last few days of November, then working through the entire month of December."

"I'm sure Sylvie and your cousins are glad to see you."

My goodness, but he smelled nice. Like man and strength and spice and something so incredibly alluring it made her want to inhale deeply and just sigh in appreciation. "The town's changed a bit." Emma had seen Sylvie at least once a year, but that usually involved her enticing her grandmother to whatever city Emma worked in. "You seem to have a lot going on. And now . . . you're mayor."

He laughed at that, the sound deep and rich. Noah stepped from behind his desk and surprised Emma by lowering his frame into the chair beside her. He was so . . . close. The room instantly shrank, as did a little bit of her confidence.

"I still have my practice in Bentonville, but I've obviously had to cut back on my work load there. It was an unfortunate event that led to my being mayor. It's just until the special election next February."

"I'm sure they picked the best man for the job. You've always loved this town."

"I still do. We have big goals. I assume Mayor Conway told you our plan to make Sugar Creek a vital tourist destination. With the boom in cultural hot spots in the surrounding towns, it's the perfect time. People like quaint, and we've got plenty of that."

"You just have to capitalize on what you have and make sure tourists know about it."

"Right. That's partly Melissa's job."

"The woman on maternity leave."

"She's done an incredible job organizing our events for the next few months. This holiday season is a critical time for us." He placed his elbow on the armrest and leaned toward her. "Why exactly do you want this job?"

"I had multiple phone meetings with the mayor. He said the job was mine."

"You didn't answer my question."

"I'm taking a little sabbatical from television. I want to spend the holidays with Sylvie, and of course, I look forward to reconnecting to my hometown." Emma leaned closer. "Noah, I can help Sugar Creek. I'd like to do a story on the way the town's celebrating Christmas and putting me on the front lines is the perfect way to make that happen. I can get Sugar Creek national promotion on *Sunrise News*. Think of the impact."

Noah studied a spot on the carpet as he considered this. "Emma, I'm going to be honest with you. I don't think you're the person for the job."

"I disagree." Had he not heard her say she could get them the attention of the whole country? "Melissa needs her time off. And coincidentally, I have about six weeks to spare. I'd say it was ideal." Minus the fact that she'd be working with her ex-fiancé.

"I'm trying to help you here. It's not anything you'd be interested in."

"I have a double major in journalism and marketing. I think I can handle the huge PR needs of a small town."

"Our PR needs are actually fairly significant now. We can't afford to drop the ball. I've put out feelers for some outside marketing assistance."

"You truly think I can't do this?"

"I think we need someone who isn't just passing through. Someone who cares about Sugar Creek."

Emma handed Noah the file in her hand. "Here are the copies of my emails with Mayor Conway, as well as a comprehensive list of ideas I have and my resume. The mayor said I had the job."

"The mayor's dead."

Emma rested her hand over her heart. "And you're not going to honor the last wish of this great man of values and integrity?"

"He died of an overdose in a pay-by-hour hotel wearing fishnets, pink underwear, and accompanied by two individuals who were neither his wife nor definitely female."

Oh. "At least the bar is set low."

"I'm not running a popularity contest. I'm trying to run a law firm and a town. I'm not sure how much Mayor Conway told you, but Sugar Creek has undergone the first phase of renovations thanks to some federal and state grants."

"The downtown area looks amazing." Gone were the derelict and empty stores. The run-down buildings had been painted vintage colors that invited shopping and gathering. Broken windows had been replaced with decorated displays that could match anything in Manhattan. Downtown Sugar Creek was a buzzing hive of restaurants, shops, and a coffee house or two. "I hear you helped make a lot of that happen."

"I'm good at paperwork."

"Like the kind you might push through to give me this job?"

Noah shifted in his seat, angling closer. "I'm pretty certain my predecessor left out some pertinent information about this temporary job he offered you."

"Are fishnets involved?"

He didn't smile. "No, but Christmas is."

"I'm aware of this. You think I can't handle some Christmas events? On *Sunrise News*, I single-handedly organized a nationwide coat drive for children, raised over three hundred thousand dollars for cancer research, and initiated a yearly marathon for—"

"Emma, I'm sure your resume is stellar. But Melissa's job is more than just throwing some punch-and-cake events at the VFW. Sugar Creek is a unique town. We have the historical battlefields, our nature offerings, and our Victorian homes. We've decided to capitalize on every aspect of the community. Do you know what people love for Christmas?"

"iTunes gift cards?"

"Small towns. Charming burgs with welcoming people." He reached across his desk for a folder of his own, pulled out a stack of papers, and handed them to her. "Sugar Creek will become a Christmas destination for travelers. We want to be their go-to Christmas village, and we're behind as it is."

Emma flipped through a few pages of the Project Christmas plans. Community tree lighting. Tour of homes. A trail of lights for visitors to drive through. Ice rink off the square, a nativity, a play at the arts center, community choral concert. The list went on and on. Things that would put Christmas spirit in anyone's heart.

Except hers.

"You hope to give people a Rockwell Christmas." She shut the folder, dropping it into her lap like it weighed a hundred pounds.

"Not hope. We *will* give them this small-town charm for Christmas. It starts immediately. The person who fills in for Melissa will live, eat, and breathe Christmas." He watched Emma closely, and it was all she could do not to gag right in front of the man.

"I can do this." And somewhere in there would be a story so inspirational, she'd get her job back.

Noah rested his hand on Emma's. "You told the world you hated Christmas on live TV."

"Mostly just the West Coast." Thanks to a time delay.

"Every citizen of this town saw it."

"That explained Silas Mooney's snubbing me on the sidewalk this morning."

"He's only been the town Santa for forty years."

"He knows he's not the real one, right?"

"See, right there. That's exactly the kind of attitude we don't need. There's too much at stake."

The job was slipping through her fingers. "No, I can do this. Give me a chance. Please, Noah."

Noah looked down at the armrest where Emma now clutched his hand. "I don't think it's in the best interest of the town."

"What about my best interests?" *Please let me stay.* "I need this chance."

"You could just go work for another news station. Do what you were trained to do."

But she couldn't. She was blacklisted. "On Christmas Eve, a star led the Wise Men to Jesus. I feel . . . I feel like I'm being led to Sugar Creek. Following . . . yonder star."

"You're really reaching here, aren't you?"

"I'm committed to this."

He lifted his eyes so slowly, so deliberately, and his voice dropped low. "And why should I believe a commitment means anything to you?"

His words were a scythe right through her battered heart. At one time this man had been her everything. "I was twenty-one years old," she said quietly. "I'm through apologizing for that."

"I didn't ask you to apologize." He rose from the chair and sat on the edge of his desk. "I asked why I should assume a commitment from you was worth anything. You don't care about this town."

"Of course I do." Granted, she needed the town to get her job back, but she did care for Sugar Creek. "It's the closest thing to a hometown I've ever had."

He scrubbed a hand over his face before turning those intense eyes back to Emma. "I'll give you two weeks. You have two weeks to not only pick up where Melissa left off, but take it a step further. Melissa had good things planned. It's your job to make them great."

She nodded furiously. "Absolutely. Consider it done."

He studied her for a moment, and Emma wondered what he saw. She was no longer the girl who wore the daily pony-tail, but the woman with chestnut hair that fell in waves down her back. Her face had a few lines, but late nights and little sleep would age anyone. Did he see that her hazel eyes still captured everything about him—his every move, his every feature? And right now—the way he wanted her gone.

"I won't let you down," Emma said. Not this time.

"It's not me you should worry about. It's an entire town."

"You can count on me to bring Christmas to Sugar Creek." She stood and held out her hand, hoping he didn't notice the way it still lightly trembled. "Do we have a deal?"

Noah captured her fingers and shook, his skin a fire on hers. "You're hired."

"Thank you. You won't regret it." She slipped her hand from his, picked up her purse, and walked toward the door.

"Emma?"

She stopped and turned, struck by the way the sun

piped through the window, illuminating his form like a holy spotlight. "Yes?"

"Don't treat this like our engagement," he said. "If you take the job, you can't just walk away from it."

Nodding, she turned her head before Noah could see the tears and walked away.

Just like she'd done all those years ago.

4

When Emma awoke the next morning, her very first thought was that she was in hell.

Her second was that she was going to kill her grandmother.

A violent alarm sounded from the hall. Not the sort that rudely jostled one awake for work, but more like the noise one might expect before a bomb struck your city.

Sylvie's voice called through a staticky microphone. "This is a drill! This is only a drill!"

As the obnoxious noises got closer, Emma let her back melt against the headboard, rested her hand on her spastic chest, and waited for the appearance of her grandmother.

"This is a test! This is only a test! Take your emergency positions."

Clothed in head-to-toe black, as if she were about to do a little midnight B&E, Sylvie opened Emma's bedroom door and slinked inside, checking to her right and left.

"There are no perps in here," Emma said.

"Hon, there are pervs everywhere."

"Did you put your hearing aide in this morning?" Emma yelled.

"No time. We need to establish your escape route should there be trouble."

"Would you put that megaphone down, for crying out loud?" Emma slapped her hand against the bedside table, searching for her phone to check the time. The darkness outside was a good hint she wasn't in danger of being late to work on her first day.

The megaphone honked like an angry goose as Sylvie set it to her lips once again. "Your phone has been confiscated. Your generation can't find your way out of a Wal-Mart parking lot without your modern devices. Now what are you going to do? There's an intruder on the first floor and a fire on the second."

Emma snatched the megaphone in a football play worthy of the Hall of Fame. "Sylvie, what time is it?"

"Oh five hundred hours."

"I don't have to be at work 'til eight."

"Danger doesn't wait until you've had your kale smoothie, Barbie doll."

The woman would never change. "I think we're pretty safe here. From . . . " What had Sylvie said? "Robbery and tornado."

Her grandmother huffed loud enough to lift the ceiling then plopped on the bed. "It was fire and intrusion."

"Right." Emma rubbed her bleary eyes and yawned. "I know retirement's hard, but you really need to get a hobby."

"I have one. Frannie and I make conceal-and-carry purses. I sent you one last Christmas."

"That hidden compartment was for a gun?"

"What did you think it was for?"

"Hiding my Snickers."

"You are absolutely your mother's child." Sylvie reached for Emma's hand and clasped it in hers. Her grandma's hand was so delicate, yet held an undeniable strength. Those hands had taken down assassins, protected dignitaries, rocked babies, and dried Emma's tears. "You don't come out of the CIA without a neurosis or two."

Right—one or two.

"I just like to make sure the ones I love are as safe as possible at all times," Sylvie said.

And Emma loved her for that. "I used to be the only girl in school who'd get a twelve-pack of Mace in her stocking."

"Santa's no dummy." Sylvie scooted right next to Emma, shoulder to shoulder. The two had spent many evenings together like this. Emma talking about school and boys. Sylvie talking about bomb detonation and bullet trajectories.

"Are you ready for your big day?"

Emma let her head fall onto Sylvie's narrow shoulder. "It feels so weird."

"What's that, Shug?"

"To be back here. To have lost my dream job."

"Temporarily lost. You'll get that back in no time. Wait 'til they hear all about our Sugar Creek Christmas. I'm telling you, this town is the perfect human interest story. America will love it." She kissed Sylvie's forehead. "And they'll love you."

"But I'm working for my ex-fiancé."

"At least he's hot. You could be looking at worse."

"The very thought is exhausting."

"I hear that sigh. That was not a 'Boy, am I pooped' sigh. That was a 'that Noah Kincaid is still one hunky dude, and my heart does a little flopsy doodle every time I see him' sigh."

"Is he dating anyone?" Emma had stopped asking about him years ago, and Sylvie had wisely stopped providing information.

"Not that I know of. He went out with our lady pharmacist for a while."

"I figured he'd be married by now."

Sylvie nudged her shoulder against Emma's. "Maybe he hasn't found the right one yet. It's not too late to try again, you know."

"No, that ship has sailed. Plus he's barely speaking to me. I'm lucky he agreed to honor the job offer."

"Of course he did. He's a good man. And you're a good girl. And I still think you'd make a couple hot as any we read about in our book club."

"Except he's not a billionaire Middle Eastern prince, and I'm not his knocked-up secretary."

"We can't all have the dream." She patted Emma's leg. "He'll warm up to you, honey. Nobody can resist my Emma."

"We're not getting back together. So don't go picking out 'his and hers' Smith & Wessons."

"I still think you should stay with me while you're here. We have so much lost time to make up for."

Sylvie had a handful of rent houses in Sugar Creek, and with one conveniently in between renters, Emma was moving in.

"We've talked about this. It will give me time to work on my story for the show, and your house won't sit vacant."

"If you stayed here, we could have a slumber party every night—eating junk food and watching true crime."

"Watching true crime is not nearly as fun when your grandmother somehow already knows every detail of the case."

Sylvie picked up Emma's hand and linked their fingers. "So I got in too late last night to share a bit of news."

"You're renouncing the NRA?"

Sylvie smiled. "Your daddy called yesterday."

Emma stilled. "Why?"

"He calls from time to time to check up on you."

"What does that mean? How often? Like weekly?"

Sylvie paused a little too long. "A few times a year."

It was something, Emma supposed. "What does he want?"

"Edward wants to talk to you. Says he doesn't have your latest number. He'd like to see you, Em."

"No."

"Hon, it's time to let it go. Don't you think?"

"He wrote a Christmas song about mom dying, dragged me all over the world like a prop, didn't care about things like my education or whether we'd stay somewhere long enough to make a friend, and cursed the world with what is the absolute worst Christmas song ever."

"He's still your dad."

"Dads don't let grandparents raise their kids." There was that old bitterness. She thought she'd taken care of that a long time ago. The hurt, the anger over being her father's afterthought, the way he'd capitalized on her mother's painful fight with the cancer that had taken her on Emma's eighth Christmas.

"I still miss her," Emma whispered.

"Me, too, Shug. God, I miss her." She squeezed Emma's hand. "But I see her in you. All the time. And she'd want you to forgive the man. Perhaps even call him once in a while."

"Maybe one day," Emma said. "But not this one."

~

IGNORING Sylvie's advice to pack heat and show cleavage, Emma made her first appearance as an employee of the city of Sugar Creek. Per her usual habit, she was fifteen minutes early and wearing her television smile.

"Good morning, Delores," Emma said, proud to recall the receptionist's name. "How are you today?"

"My bunions are killing me, and my kid wants a toy that can't be found except by scalpers."

"Oh, I'm sorry. Um, I'm not sure if you remember me from yesterday—"

"I know who you are. Hope all our Christmas stuff doesn't offend you."

Emma blinked. "I think the town's plans are lovely."

Delores planted her elbows on her desk and her voice dipped John Wayne low. "If you touch that baby Jesus in the manger on the square, I will find you. You feeling me?"

"I believe so." Emma searched in vain for the appearance of a friendly face. Or anyone's face but Delores's. "Is Noah here?" "That's Mr. Kincaid to you."

Emma didn't bother telling the woman that she had been months away from being *Mrs.* Kincaid, and she was not calling any man who had seen her in granny panties and head gear *mister*.

"He's in a meeting. Told me to show you to your office."

Now we're talking. "Great."

Delores pointed her chewed Bic to the left.

"That first door there?" Emma asked.

"You're the fancy reporter. I'll let you figure it out."

Her camera smile wobbling, Emma tried the first door. Inside she found two bookshelves, a wall of file cabinets, and a desk with one picture of Melissa, her husband, and a border collie. She had to be in the right place.

Emma opened the blinds and looked out. The office had

a perfect view of the entire town square. Early morning joggers braved the cold, while two school buses took their turns at the four-way stop. A few professionally dressed folks walked into Benton's Coffee House, an establishment that looked brand new. The sky was a web of gray clouds that stretched over the top of the city. Sylvie had said something about a chance of snow this morning, but it was only late November. The town rarely saw the white stuff so soon.

"I see you found your office."

Emma turned at that achingly familiar voice.

Noah stood in the doorway, more out than in, as if he feared stepping into her new territory.

"Yes. The square looks great, by the way. It's really developed."

"The lighting of the square is a big event for us. It's a week from Thursday. I assume you've opened your email and checked the agenda I sent you."

Emma bit back a snippy response and just smiled through gritted teeth. "I'll do that right now."

"The Trail of Lights begins tomorrow night. You'll need to contact everyone on the list and confirm their participation. Brief me on that within the hour. Give them the details for the run-through tonight. I'll need you to confirm the caterer for the gala next month, the children's choir for the tree lighting ceremony, Santa for the children's fest, and—"

"Noah—" Emma crossed the floor and stood in front of him. "I'm here to do the job, and I'll do it. You're already expecting me to screw this up."

"I do not think you're going to—"

"Yes, you do. I'm sorry you have no faith in me, but I can do this. You want a dry run of the Trail of Lights tonight, and that's what you'll get. Just leave it to me."

He checked his phone, already dismissing her. "I won't

be available all day. If you have a problem or a question, ask Delores."

"Are you unavailable to me just today or will this be a normal thing?"

Noah's eyes briefly held hers. "Run everything through my assistant."

Emma watched the man she once loved walk away. She knew he had a right to be mad at her. But they had to work together. Surely he could be civil?

The rest of the day flew by with phone calls and emails. The Trail of Lights was not just a few streets of town. Over 200 homes had signed up to participate. According to Melissa's notes, the lights would begin on the bridge over the creek, then snake through the town. The trail included everything from a simple outlining of a home in white lights to a professionally designed holiday display. Homes, businesses, and even organizations would be setting up displays on empty spots at the park. Food and drink trailers would be open late for the tourists, luring them in with lattes, cocoa, and an evening snack.

As Emma worked at her desk, fingers flying over the keyboard and phone pressed to her ear, she kept an eye on the door across the hall.

Noah never returned to check on her. Didn't inquire about her plans for lunch or how she was getting along. Any questions Emma had, she grudgingly presented to Delores, who answered in her own Morse code of grunts and shrugs.

Yet it wasn't as if Noah had totally disappeared.

Emma could hear him, even occasionally see him in the lobby from her desk. He laughed with Delores. He shot the bull with the county judge who stopped by. He was Mr. Good Humor to the ministerial alliance that dropped in to discuss the tree lighting ceremony. From the UPS guy to the old man who made an appointment just to complain about rising cable costs, Noah was the epitome of charm and charisma.

At five o'clock, she heard him tell his secretary goodbye.

Emma expected him to pop his head in and give her the same courtesy.

But Noah left without a word.

From her office window, she watched him climb into his truck and drive away.

It was better this way. The less contact, the easier it would be to leave at the first of the year.

But if that was best. . . why did she feel as bleak as that wintery sky?

5

That night Sylvie stood in the living room of her rental house on Harrison Avenue holding a hot pink pistol. “This house doesn’t have an electronic security system, but I got your security right here.”

“Put that gun away. I don’t even know how to use it.” Emma rolled her two suitcases in and surveyed the house.

“Have you forgotten everything I’ve taught you?”

“Yes. In therapy.”

This small Queen Anne of Sylvie’s had been completely renovated. Dark hard woods, granite in the kitchen, a marble-tiled fireplace. Old trim work still outlined the doors and windows, and some of the original light fixtures and glass doorknobs remained. The home brimmed with charm. It invited you to settle in and stay a long while. Like years.

Emma pulled herself from her white-picket thoughts. “I still want to pay you rent.”

“Don’t be ridiculous. My next tenant isn’t due for a few months. It’s perfect. Unless you’re planning on trashing it with your wild parties.”

"No wild parties for me."

"Pity," she said. "I was hoping for an invite."

Sylvie slipped the gun back in her concealed holster. "Frannie and I are on neighborhood watch, so we'll drive by at least once every single night."

"Most grandmothers would just bring over a casserole."

"You have no ideas the dangers that lurk out there."

"I read the Sugar Creek paper this morning. The worst thing in the police report was an escaped cow walking down Lee Town."

"Sometimes cows are just walking bombs. Once I was in Egypt and—"

"Sylvie, I don't want to know!" Emma plugged her ears and walked toward the kitchen.

"So you were telling me how work went," Sylvie called. "Did Noah pin you against the desk or leave you dirty voice mails?"

"He's not even talking to me."

Her grandmother joined her in the kitchen. "Shug, he just needs time. You're a hard thing to get over." She gave a gentle wink. "Or maybe you don't want him over you?"

"Of course I do. I don't want to work with him for six weeks with him being all mean and broody." Especially while he was his usual charming self to everyone else. Even the annoying citizens. Like his secretary.

Sylvie leaned against the counter and leveled those sharp-shooter eyes on her granddaughter. "Does seeing him again bring back any old feelings?"

Emma opened her mouth to fire off a quippy barb, but the words fizzled and popped. "Yes. I didn't expect that. But he's still . . . Noah. Even when he's totally ignoring me he has the power to make my heart beat faster and my breath catch. I still smile at the sound of his laugh. He's still the most handsome guy I've ever laid eyes on."

"Have you considered that maybe you still love—"

They both jumped at the sound of a throat clearing.

Emma turned to find Noah standing in the living room, hands stuffed in his pockets, his face the neutral mask he had worn that morning. "Hi." His eyes locked on Emma. "I knocked a few times, but I guess you didn't hear me."

"No, we didn't," Emma said, eyes wide. How long had he been standing there?

"Come on in here, you cute thing, you!" With a pointed look at her granddaughter, Sylvie breezed into the living room and pulled Noah into a hug. "Don't you look just like a Ralph Lauren ad?"

Did he ever. Noah had changed out of his business attire into dark jeans and a sweater. With those eyes, that jaw, and that athlete's body, he could easily have stepped out of the pages of a magazine.

"I hear we're going to have quite the light show." Sylvie gave his back a maternal pat. "I'll have to wear one of those blackout masks to bed."

Noah kissed Sylvie's blushed cheek. "That's gonna make it hard for you to sleep with one eye open."

"You know me too well," she said. "My ninja senses won't let me down. I think all the lights will only help my neighborhood watch."

"You mean neighborhood neurotic snooping," Emma said.

"I broke up some gang activity at Delphie Martin's place just last week."

Noah finally smiled. "You told me it was a pack of raccoons."

Sylvie lifted her chin. "They are not to be underestimated either. Do you have any idea what they can do with those little thumbs? Terrorists, all of them."

Noah and her grandmother made small talk about folks they knew, while Emma stood in the background, about as noticeable as the small gossamer spider web hanging over the fireplace. As she watched Noah smile and laugh with Sylvie, Emma suddenly knew what she wanted for Christmas more than anything. She wanted Noah's forgiveness. Yes, he had a right to be angry. But it had been ten years. They were both different people now. Surely he could find it in his heart to accept one of the one hundred apologies she had sent his way. Emma craved it like water in her desert.

"I saw your rental car, Emma."

Noah's voice pulled Emma from her pitiful ruminations. Was he actually speaking to *her?*

"Are you moving in here?" he asked.

"Yes," she said. "Sylvie's just cased the joint and declared it fit to inhabit."

"It's a good neighborhood," Sylvie said. "I'm just going to step into the kitchen and unpack some of the stuff I brought."

"Did your grandmother tell you who lives across the street?" Noah closed the distance between him and Emma.

"The two-story sage green house with the wrap-around porch?"

"Rebuilt the porch myself."

"You're my neighbor?"

"I take it Sylvie left out that part."

Emma looked back into the kitchen, where her grandmother hummed a little too loudly. "Speaking of terrorists."

She wondered what Noah thought about his new neighbor. Would it really be so bad for him to have to live across the street from her? "Look, I'm only going to be here a short while. You won't have to worry about me bothering you or peeping in the windows while you're entertaining a date."

Noah's lips quirked. "Is that my cue to make the same promise?"

Emma laughed. "Do you remember that time you climbed the trellis of my sorority to my second-story bedroom?"

"Or what I thought was your bedroom."

"The cleaning lady thought it was very romantic."

"After she called 9-1-1."

Sometimes the past was so sweet, it hurt to revisit. "We had some good times."

He slowly nodded. "We did."

Emma's breath caught as Noah watched her, saying nothing. He was so close, she could see the gold flecks in his brown eyes.

"Noah, I wanted to tell you—"

But his words overran hers, shoving them both away from the oncoming train of old memories. "I'm actually here on business tonight."

"Oh." A definite mood breaker. "What's up?"

"We need to go for a little drive."

He didn't sound the least bit happy about it. "Is there a body bag and some duct tape in your trunk by chance?"

"We're going to do a dry run of the lights tour."

"That was next on my evening agenda. We just dropped some stuff off here first. Sylvie and I are going."

"Emma!" As if on cue, Sylvie buzzed out of the kitchen like an angry bee. "I gotta bail on our little moonlit drive.

Frannie just called, and she has a code ten emergency at her house."

It was impossible to keep up with all of Sylvie's lingo. "Is that a stray dog or a suspicious noise?"

"It means she needs someone to color her roots." She gave a loud, enthusiastic kiss on Emma's cheek, then reached up to Noah and cupped his face in her hands. "You take care of my Emma here, okay? Don't let her go out into the big city all by herself."

Before Emma could protest, Sylvie was gone.

Leaving Emma and Noah standing alone in the living room. Again.

"I'll drive." Noah jerked his chin toward the door. "My truck's still running."

He wasn't asking her to go to spend time with her. Noah didn't trust her to do this simple task. "I'd rather check out the lights myself."

"I want this done right."

The hurt flashed on her face before she could school her features. "I'm pretty capable of driving through town and making sure everyone has their lights up."

"Really?" He reached for her hand and led her out the front door. "Did you happen to notice your house is on the tour?"

"I just got to town." Emma stopped beneath the glow of her porch light. "I need a few days to organize that. It's not like I got on the airplane with a two-story ladder and some LEDs."

"The tour opens Monday night. We need everyone ready, and that includes your home."

Another detail Sylvie forgot to mention. "I'd rather drive alone. You can text me your Christmas light thoughts and innermost feelings."

"Get in the truck."

She slammed the door closed behind her and locked it tightly. "Pretty sure this constitutes as employee harassment. I'm going to consider suing."

He opened her car door and smiled. "Let me know if you need an attorney referral."

6

Holy sleigh bells, Noah smelled good.

There was something about being confined to a truck cab that just encapsulated and intensified the scent of a man. Noah's scent was clean, rugged, with a hint of woodsy spice.

With barely a glance in her direction, he buckled his seatbelt, flicked on her seat warmer, and pulled onto the road. "We'll start at the bridge, just like the tourists."

"Exactly what I was going to do."

"Mr. Dennis always has a light show, and you gotta make sure it doesn't blind the oncoming traffic coming around that corner on Lee Town."

"Melissa left a stack of notes on this. I was going to check that."

That earned her a grunt, and Noah didn't try to make conversation until they passed the bridge that connected Sugar Creek to Bentonville. He turned around in a driveway and faced his hometown.

"I assume we're waiting for nine o'clock," Emma said.

"Unless you called every one of the participants and changed the time I told them."

"I might've called a few," Noah admitted. "But I didn't change a thing." He glanced at the clock on his dash, and with no one behind them, he put the truck in park and let it idle.

Emma studied Noah's face in the dark and wondered what the man was thinking as he stared out into the night. "So . . . how's your mama?"

"Fine." He searched the sky, as if making sure all the constellations were hanging in their correct spots.

"And your dad?"

"He's well."

It was clear his family wouldn't be nominating him to compose the Kincaid Christmas newsletter.

"Cassiopeia is bright tonight," Emma said quietly.

At that, Noah turned and met her gaze, holding it so long, Emma had to remind herself to breathe.

"Do you remember our first date?" she asked.

He was silent, so silent, she didn't think he was going to answer. Then finally Noah cleared his throat, as if reluctant to verbalize the memory. "The college planetarium."

"You talked your friend into letting us have a picnic there. I think that was the most romantic date I've ever been on."

His laugh sounded hollow. "You've been all over the world."

And yet nothing compared to the memories she'd had with Noah. "You had some pretty good moves for a frat boy. Remember when you leaned over me to show me Ursa Major?" She unbuckled her seatbelt, pointed her finger high, and leaned into Noah, aiming her arm across his body.

"It's somewhere over there," you said. "To the left. A little more. See it?" Emma laughed at the memory.

"You never did see it," he said near her ear.

Emma turned her head, her face so near Noah's. "I just pretended not to." *My stars, he's gorgeous.* "You weren't the only one with some game."

His smile was slow, a slight tug of his lips. "I remember that date got me to first base."

Emma couldn't seem to move away.

His eyes dipped to her lips, and the words *kiss me* crashed through Emma like a heavy chorus. The air in the truck sparked and sizzled with the energy between them. Whatever had been there over ten years ago, something remained.

Noah turned his head just slightly, his lips now hovering over hers—waiting, teasing, considering.

Emma closed the small gap and feathered her mouth over his.

Suddenly the truck lit up, as if someone had flipped a switch, and Noah immediately pulled away.

He rubbed the back of his neck and returned his attention to the town, now illuminated like a Christmas dream. "Nine o'clock on the dot."

Emma's lips still tingling, her senses humming from the kiss that barely qualified, she straightened in her seat and watched the light show.

It really was beautiful.

The white lights dominated, beginning first on the bridge, as if pointing the way to a magical land just beyond the creek. Nestled in the trees and rural vista, the homes sparkled and flickered with their displays.

"That's my home." Noah's voice held the kind of reverence reserved for art hanging in the Guggenheim.

"It's a great town."

"Great? You can look at that countryside right there, and great is all you see?"

"I'm sorry." Suddenly her seatbelt seemed a little choking. "Perhaps the two-second kiss seemed to have robbed me of adjectives."

"That wasn't a kiss."

"Oh." She'd just *had* to mention it. "Whatever you call that. A fleeting and accidental meeting of the lips."

"Which I believe you initiated."

"There was a definite lean on your part."

"I wasn't leaning." His grin deepened. "Just like when we were in college—you can't keep your hands off me."

"I was—" Emma's cheeks burned hotter than coals from a stove. "Never mind. You're right, that was not a kiss. I'm sorry if I invaded your space while strolling down memory lane." Tripping down memory lane. Falling flat on her humiliated face onto memory lane.

His sigh sounded as weary as she felt. "I'm not interested in rekindling any relationship with you," he said.

"That makes two of us."

"You're just passing through."

She crossed her arms over her chest. "Yep."

Noah jerked the truck into drive and drove them across the bridge and into town. The creek flowed beneath them, shimmering with the reflection of the town lights. Large red and white candy canes blinked from streetlights as they entered the first neighborhood. Glowing icicles hanging from rooftops, trees wrapped in lights in front yards, snow men dancing, a nativity at Pastor Joe's, animated reindeer at Mr. and Mrs. Simpsons', a laser show at Miles Tisdale's. Each house was so different, yet each so achingly lovely. Not one person on the trail did anything less than a huge production. The old Victorian homes looked so regal accentuated by all the lights.

It beat even Rockefeller Plaza.

Sugar Creek, you have gone and turned my head.

They passed a two-story home with gingerbread boys and girls dancing around giant gumdrops that towered all the way to the roof.

"You've done an incredible job," Emma said, still slightly embarrassed she had kissed Noah. What had possessed her?

"Any success the town has this season is thanks to a team effort."

She'd read Melissa's notes. She knew how much Noah had been involved, even before he'd stepped in as mayor. They drove for another half hour in silence, save for the occasional observation Noah wanted Emma to record.

Two hours later, Noah circled back to Emma's house and pulled into her drive.

"The town looks incredible." It would film beautifully for the morning show story. Her producer would love it. "Wait, what are you doing?" She watched Noah jump out of the truck and walk around to her side.

"I'm walking you to your door. Don't your big city men do this?"

City men didn't do anything the way this man did. His mama had raised him right. "Thank you." She took his outstretched hand and stepped down onto the driveway. It was no surprise that he dropped her hand, but the twang of regret that followed left Emma unsettled. Surely it was just the season. The holidays always made her lonely.

They stopped at her front door, and Noah held out his hand for her keys.

She simply stood there in the frigid night air and

watched him. "Are you going to be mad at me the entire time I'm in town?"

"I hope to not be that aware of you."

The memory of their interrupted kiss flashed through Emma's mind. "Let me know how that goes for you. But I'm invested in this for the duration of Melissa's maternity leave." Like she needed to remind him one more time that she wouldn't bail.

Noah stepped closer. "Hand me your keys."

"I'll let myself in." Her words came out in ghostly puffs. "I had a lovely evening. I'll contact the homeowners you suggested first thing in the morning. Good night."

"There's a storm coming, you know."

Pretty much one brewing right here between us. "Sylvie's already warned me. It's going to get cold, chance of light wintery precip, stock up on milk and bread, and change all my internet passwords."

"Do you have fire wood?"

"Not yet."

"Has Sylvie had the heater checked in a while?"

"I have no idea. She was probably too busy at the shooting range."

Noah scratched at the stubble that flecked his jaw. "When's the last time she had your chimney cleaned?"

"That sounds very personal."

There was the sighing thing again. "Open the door, Emma."

So she did.

It was strange to see him among her things and in her space once again. The small living room seemed to shrink as soon as he stepped into it. After requesting a flashlight, Noah walked to the fireplace and shined the beam into the chimney.

"It's too dark to tell, but I'm pretty sure you've got a bird's nest or something up there." Noah stepped away from the fireplace. "Call Sid Tucker tomorrow. Tell him I sent you and to put you on his priority list."

"Yes, sir."

Noah took another glance around, frowning at the two camping chairs stationed in her living room like a parlor seating area. "You could at least get a couch."

"I'll put that on my to-do list as well." Seeing him in her rental home, it reminded her of the plans the two of them had made. Or rather the plans Noah had made. He'd had their apartment all picked out. After they got married, they would live there while he finished law school. Then move back to Sugar Creek.

He had returned as planned.

She had gone anywhere but Arkansas.

"Good night, Emma."

"Noah?" Emma followed him to the front door. "I enjoyed seeing Sugar Creek with you tonight."

"The town's finally becoming what it was supposed to be." Noah's gaze lingered on Emma's. "It was there all along."

"I guess it just needed you."

A flicker of warmth lit Noah's eyes. "Good night, Emma."

"I'll see you—" Emma's words halted at the new focus of Noah's attention.

He pointed above them. There over the door dangled a bouquet of mistletoe. "What is that?"

Oh, geez. "My guess is Sylvie's version of a house-warming gift." She could've sent a bundt cake.

"Knowing your grandma, there's probably a spy cam in it."

Nerves ignited, Emma laughed. "Pretty sure we can count on that."

Noah took one step, placing him toe-to-toe with Emma. His eyes held hers for the span of two slow breaths. He reached out and ran a hand over Emma's hair, letting those gentle fingers stop at her cheek. "I'd hate to disappoint her." He pulled her close.

Emma stepped into him, slid her hands up his chest, and let her lips part.

Only to feel the press of his mouth to her cheek.

She closed her eyes. Disappointment, regret, desire. All these things flamed within her, threatening to invite the tears. Noah was no longer hers. She had walked away years ago, and he had never forgiven her.

"Good night, boss." She patted the chest beneath her hands and stepped back. She expected to find his gaze full of mirth, teasing. *Wasn't it cute? She had thought he was truly going to kiss her.*

But his darkened expression held no humor.

Without a word, Noah turned and walked away.

The cold battering against her coat, Emma stood there and watched him go.

"Emma?" Noah stopped in the driveway and turned around.

"Yes?"

"When I kiss you"—he opened his door, and light spilled onto the pavement—"there won't be any doubt."

7

"Fancy Pants has *rhinopneumonitis*." Delores stood at Emma's desk, her frown extra scowly.

Emma hit *send* on an email. "Well, then I guess you should get your husband some antibiotics."

"Fancy Pants is your horse. One of the two you'll be needing for your sleigh rides."

Oh, no. This was very bad. This horse couldn't be sick. How could he just quit on her? "What's *rhinopneumonitis*?"

"I have no idea," the secretary drawled. "Let me go check my horse disease dictionary."

This woman was so getting coal for Christmas.

"I can tell you it means he won't be able to drive a sleigh for at least a week. That's what his owner said."

"Where am I going to get a replacement?" Emma flopped her sandwich onto her paper plate, no longer hungry for lunch. "The sleigh rides start tomorrow."

"That's what they pay you big bucks for." Delores's sarcastic tone was as impressive as her eye roll. "I'm sure you'll figure something out."

"Could you maybe get me a list of—"

"No." She marched heavy-footed to the door. "You're not the only one with urgent things to do."

Ten minutes later on her way to the break room, Emma walked past an overworked Delores filing her nails and checking *General Hospital* spoilers. Emma held her tongue, clutched her empty coffee mug, and tromped down the hall for a much-needed refill.

"Something wrong?"

Emma's spoon stopped its rotation in her mug, and she turned at Noah's voice. "Are you actually speaking to me?"

"I speak to you all the time."

She added creamer. "I think you have me mixed up with every other member of the Sugar Creek population."

Noah walked by her and opened the white refrigerator. Today he wore dark khakis, topping it off with a navy shirt he filled out quite nicely. She would be content to stare at him all day. Especially in lieu of finding livery.

"I asked you if something's wrong," he repeated.

"No. Nothing." Except the fact that she had a sleigh with no horse. She had called all over the county, and nobody had a horse that could fill in. The task was proving to be more difficult than she'd imagined. It was the one thing you couldn't just order up from the internet.

"Are you sure about that?" Noah placed a bowl of soup in the microwave.

"Uh-huh."

"You realize you just put your seventh sugar packet in your coffee."

She looked down. There was a tiny graveyard of crumbled white packs all around her cup. "I'm just a little distracted."

Noah leaned against the granite counter. "You always were so edgy at Christmas."

"Statistics tell us that most Americans are." Emma knew her uppity tone sounded completely ridiculous.

"But you're kind of off the charts. It has to be hard to be in over your head with our Christmas plans while disliking the holiday so much."

"I'm not in over my head. I'm totally fine. I can handle this. The city light tour worked beautifully, didn't it?"

"Of course."

And he hadn't said *thank you* or *good job* or anything. As usual he had barely spoken to her at all. "I know you're probably breaking out in hives from what has to be our longest conversation since I started here, so I'll just get back to my office and get out of your way."

"Emma, wait."

He lightly caught her wrist. "I'm sorry if I've been—" He seemed to be scanning his mind for just the right word—"unavailable."

And what a word it was. As in *"I'm not here as your boss, and I'm sure not available to you in any other capacity you might be dreaming of."*

Because Emma was. Dreaming of him.

And she was thinking of him way too much.

I miss your laugh, your face smiling at mine. I'm sorry I messed up so badly all those years ago.

Last night she had dreamed she was stranded on a Caribbean beach, and he had walked across the sand, appearing out of nowhere, bringing her all sorts of sexy distractions.

And pizza. But that part of the dream wasn't really important. The point was she needed to stop these runaway fantasy thoughts about Noah. They didn't have a future. He didn't even like her.

"You know you're always welcome to stop by my office if you need something."

"Oh. Thank you."

"Just make an appointment with Delores." He turned back to his microwave. "She'll put it on my schedule."

He and Delores deserved each other. "I can handle this job on my own," Emma said. "Don't worry about it. I know you're a *very* busy man."

A fresh cup of coffee in hand, Emma stormed back through the lobby, but her steps faltered as the Christmas music wafted from Delores's speakers.

"Her life was never the same, for overnight the angels came. And I'll never forget a child's Christmas tears . . . "

"Turn it off." Not caring one whit about personal space, Emma snaked behind Delores's U-shaped desk and grabbed the woman's hot pink mouse.

"Hey!" Delores smacked Emma's hand. "Leggo my computer. You can't do that." Delores tried to edge Emma out with her voluptuous hip, but Emma had anger and adrenaline on her side.

"I'm finding another song." Which of the twenty tabs was the music on?

"That is a good tune, and you have no right to—I said get your manicured mitts off!"

"The angels cried, when they arrived that night. . . "

The computer would not cooperate. Where was Sylvie's gun when she needed it?

"Stop it!" Delores cried. "You're bringing shame to Christmas! That song is about a loving father having to watch his daughter—"

"You have *no idea* what that stupid song is about." She closed out all of Delores's screens until the music died. "That happens to be the worst holiday song ever created.

What kind of person likes that sort of thing—*Merry Christmas, your mom is dead*?"

"I like it," Delores snarled. "Now move away from my desk right now or I'll—"

"I don't want to hear that song, for the love of—"

"Emma."

She turned and bumped right into Noah. He stood so close, her chin grazed his tie.

He looked down his straight nose and lifted a brow. "You have an audience."

Suddenly aware of the surroundings, Emma was appalled to see the crowd in the lobby, waiting to see what the crazy news lady would do next. A couple of wide-eyed homeschooling mothers gathered their field-tripping charges close. Two city council members stood frozen at the water cooler, and if Emma was seeing it correctly, the city clerk was recording it all with her phone.

Noah pried the computer mouse from Emma's grip and handed it back to his secretary. "No music today, please."

Delores head bobbed with attitude. "But she—"

"That will be all, Delores."

"But I like that song and—"

"Why don't you take a break," Noah suggested to his secretary.

Her lips thinned. "I already had 'em both."

"You've worked so hard," Noah said calmly. "I think you deserve another."

The woman glowered at Emma as she reached for her purse. "You're lucky I don't sue you."

"Do not even think of responding," Noah whispered into Emma's ear. His hand clasping Emma's, Noah aimed that boyish grin at the small congregation. "Just a little Christmas stress."

A curly-headed five year-old pulled a sucker out of his mouth and pointed it at Emma. "You're gonna be on Santa's naughty list."

Oh, geez. She'd just had a total meltdown in public. Over that pathetic song. She was years past that sort of thing. But it had also been years since she'd heard it. "I'm fine." Emma took a step away from Noah. "I'm sorry."

Her feet couldn't carry her fast enough into her office, where she shut herself inside and went back to her call list for one blasted horse. When the hot tears fell like raindrops on her desk, Emma dashed them away and tried to think of better days. As soon as she turned in her pitch for the story on Sugar Creek, she would have her job back. The fun interviews. The glamour of New York. The camaraderie of her television family.

The three-thirty wake-up times. The ratings stress. The endless airplane rides. Her hair always having to be perfect. An existence without carbs. It would be back to a life without Sylvie and her cousins, and . . . without Noah.

Emma was being silly. Of course she wanted that job back. Between being back in Sugar Creek, the holidays, and spending so much time near Noah, her head was simply addled. She needed to get away from him before that dangerous rope of attraction completely wrapped around her once again and pulled her in. Even in his frosty mood, she was a puddle of irrational want. It was better that he ignored her.

At five o'clock Emma had exhausted every avenue she knew of to find a horse.

She shut her laptop, closed her eyes, and rested her forehead on the desk.

When she heard the knock at her door, she didn't even rouse. They could go away. Why would anyone want to talk to her anyway? She was the great Christmas organizing failure. Foiled by a horse with a problem she couldn't even pronounce.

More knocking from the other side of the door.

"Go away," she mumbled. "I have too much to do. Like writing my resignation letter."

"Quitting already?"

Emma jolted to attention in her chair. "Noah." She pulled a chunk of hair from her lips. "I didn't hear you come in."

The man had the nerve to smile. "Grab your coat."

"And clear out my desk?"

"No."

"What am I doing?"

"You're going with me to check on a donkey."

"Did Delores have car trouble?"

She heard his faint chuckle. "We're going to Sherman Turner's farm and getting you a replacement for your sick horse."

"You knew about that?"

He pulled her coat from her chair and held it out. "You should've asked me for help."

With Noah's help, Emma eased into her sleeves and felt her breath hitch when he picked up her red plaid scarf and draped it behind her neck and held the ends.

"Emma?"

"Yes?" She stared at his hands on her scarf.

"I'm sorry."

At that she looked up, right into his deep chocolate eyes. "What for?"

"For being a jerk."

If this was the part in the conversation where she was supposed to disagree, she wasn't going to.

"I have been avoiding you," Noah admitted. "This afternoon I waited for you to come to me for help, but you weren't going to, were you?"

"No."

"What happened between us was a long time ago." He let the words hang between them for a moment. "And even though I would've picked someone a little more pro-Christmas for Melissa's replacement, you're doing a good job. If we're going to make Sugar Creek a holiday destination, we've got to work as a team. I realized today, I'm the one not letting that happen. So . . . I'm sorry."

Her lips lifted slowly. "And I'm sorry I attacked your secretary's computer."

Noah offered her his arm. "Let's go fix this carriage situation."

She slipped her hand into the crook of his elbow, and together they walked outside into the darkened evening. Emma's heart a little lighter, she leaned into Noah as the wind brushed against them. She didn't know what he had planned to fix the no-show horse. But she felt confident that whatever he had come up with, it would work.

If only Noah could fix everything else in her life.

8

"So technically it was a mule." Noah drove his truck away from Sherman Turner's farm on a dirt road dotted with pot holes.

"Who can tell them apart?" Emma liked the way Noah bypassed the Christmas music on the radio and put on some up-beat country.

"Sherman Turner can." Noah dimmed his brights for a passing Ford.

Mr. Turner was the father of an old high school friend of Emma's. Emma and Breanne Turner had both played trumpet in the band and struggled through two years of debate. When Noah had called the man and told him Emma needed help, Sherman had only been too happy to oblige. He and Emma had caught up on life, while Noah visited with the animals. They had left Sherman's with some free range eggs, two gallons of raw milk, and a dozen stories of Breanne's kids. But most importantly, they'd gotten Sherman's guarantee that his mule would be ready to pull a carriage through town at six o'clock tomorrow.

"It'll work." Noah gave her knee a gentle shake. "Cross this off your stress list."

"I'm just a little out of my league with the livestock details."

"I have one more stop to make, then I'll take you back."

"John Darcy is meeting me with his one good working horse, and we're going to do a dry run with the carriage." Emma watched Noah in the dark cab while a weather report called for rain later in the week. "Sylvie and Frannie were going to go on the carriage ride with me, but they bailed on account of some secret call with the Secretary of Defense. Would you . . . " The skin beneath Emma's scarf flushed hot. "Would you want to go?"

Noah's voice rang with disbelief. "Seriously?"

"Right, stupid idea. I know. I was just thinking after that 'Go Team' speech you gave me today that you might want to—no, but you're right. I'll totally do the—I mean, forget I even asked, right?" Emma wanted to yank open the truck door and jump into a stampeding herd of cows. Except they all seemed to be gone for the night, and Noah wasn't driving fast enough to propel her further than the barbed-wire fence lining the road.

"No," Noah said. "I mean your grandma's seriously still talking to the government?"

"Oh." He hadn't outright rejected her. But still—what had possessed her to ask Noah to go on the carriage ride? "Um . . . yes, I believe she is. She told me the call was with her insurance agent, but I don't think she needs two burner phones for that conversation." Emma stared out the window, letting her other question drop. Maybe he would forget she asked. Or maybe his forgetting to acknowledge it was his way of brushing her off. Or maybe—

"I'm definitely in for the carriage ride." Noah maneuvered the truck through a hole big enough to mess up a tire. "Let me take something to the Henderson family, then we'll be on our way."

As Emma tapped her foot to the radio and wondered where her plan to avoid Noah had derailed, he drove a few miles east to another set of dirt roads. He pulled into the rutted driveway of a single-wide trailer, where three large dogs with aerodynamic tails roused from the wooden ramp leading to the front door.

"I'll be right back."

He hopped out, and a blast of cold air filled the truck before he shut the door. Noah dropped the tailgate and carried two children's bicycles to a nearby shed. A man in a ball cap and coveralls stepped out of the house, threw his hand up in a wave, and joined Noah. Emma watched the man fling open the crooked door to the shed, then take one bicycle and disappear inside. Noah handed him the other before the man locked the building with a padlock and patted Noah on the back. The two men laughed over something then chatted for a few minutes more. A utility light illuminated the yard, and Emma could see the man's smile from her seat in the truck.

"You ready to go?" Noah asked as he climbed back inside, smelling like wood stove and outdoors.

Emma's smile stretched her warm cheeks.

"What?" Noah stared at the dirt road ahead of them.

"Did you just drop off a few early Christmas presents to that family?"

He drove past a well-lit barn where one of the town veterinarians looked to be paying a call. "Are you hungry? Luis's taco truck has excellent carne asada."

"You're not going to answer me?"

Noah tapped the steering wheel to the beat of a radio song. "Let's just call it a Christmas secret."

"You're a good man, Noah Kincaid." She was nearly undone with the urge to touch him, to place her hands in his and assure herself he was this kind, this real.

Emma could recall the exact moment she'd known she was in love with Noah. Then less than a year later, she'd given back his ring.

But had she ever gotten back her heart?

HEAVEN WAS some authentic Mexican food— shared with the most handsome man in Sugar Creek.

Emma bit into her carne asada street taco and didn't bother to squelch her moan. "So good." She found Noah watching her lips, and Emma's skin beneath her coat warmed, despite the cutting wind. "Do I have something on my mouth?"

He reached out and rubbed his thumb over her bottom lip. "No," he said roughly.

"Mr. Kincaid, ready when you are!"

A horse whinnied behind the couple, breaking the magic cocoon that had spun around them.

"I'll be your driver tonight." Coley Biler patted his chestnut's neck. "Kanye here is a fine horse. He's ready for his debut. And Jay-Z will be back in tip-top shape next week, I know it."

Noah pulled his eyes away from Emma and shook the man's hand. As the two traded niceties, Emma zipped her coat and wondered if Noah had been about to kiss her. Definitely not on her plan to keep her distance. But when Noah Kincaid looked at her like that, she was ready to surrender anything he wanted. It was getting harder and harder to tell her heart no.

Did she even want to?

"Emma?" Noah held out his hand, and she realized he'd called her name more than once.

"Oh, right. Here we go." She placed her gloved fingers in his and stepped into a beautiful covered carriage that could seat four people in its cushioned seats behind Coley's driver's box.

Noah settled in beside Emma and pulled a red tartan blanket over their laps. Coley shouted a command to the horse, and the carriage lurched into motion. They drove for a few moments in silence, the wind blowing against them. Occasionally their jovial driver would offer a piece of trivia about a landmark, pointing out the location for the tree-lighting ceremony or the spot where a famous Civil War general had been born.

Though Emma wore her heavy winter clothing, the cold still pressed in. The nightly temperatures had been falling, and tonight's low was in the thirties. Sherman Turner had told them he believed from watching his cattle that the fore-casted rain would turn into snow. As much as Emma loved a good snow, she found she didn't want even one of Sugar Creek's Christmas activities cancelled.

"You're shivering." Noah curled his strong arm around Emma's shoulders and pulled her to him. "Do you want my coat?"

"No." She nestled into his side and watched the lights go by. "I'm feeling warmer already." Good gosh, she was weak. But moonlight, a carriage ride, and Noah holding her close? There was no way she could resist.

"Are we showing you the better side of Christmas yet?" Noah asked.

She smiled at that. "The lights and carriage ride have been nice."

His hand stroked up and down her arm. "Would you like to tell me how it is you're thirty-one years old and still go violent when you hear that song of your dad's?"

"I hadn't heard it in so long." Emma sighed. "My job doesn't exactly lend itself to me celebrating traditional holidays. I try not to go in stores during this time. I avoid holiday parties, and I pretty much just work and hibernate for the two month fest of tidings and joy." Except now Christmas practically started the day after Halloween, so she'd really had to up her avoidance strategy.

"It obviously still hurts."

"It's just this visceral reaction, you know?"

"Oh, I know. I saw it."

"I don't understand how something that celebrates my mother's death could be held up as a holiday hymn. It disgusts me."

"The song . . . or your father."

"Yes," Emma said. "All of it."

"Melissa tried to get your dad to headline our gala."

"The benefit?" She had read about the late-December gala in Melissa's notes. It was the third year they'd had a formal evening of dinner and a concert to raise money for the events for the following Christmas. Emma had seen the budget report. Turning Sugar Creek into a holiday oasis was not cheap.

"Your dad said he regretfully declined." Noah silently pointed out a house outlined in pink lights. "I take it the agreement is still in place."

"He still honors it." When Sylvie had taken legal custody, part of the settlement had included a signed promise by her father that he would never perform in Sugar

Creek. "I'm sure the agreement is now a worthless piece of paper, but my dad has stood by it. I am grateful to him for that."

"Do you ever see him?"

"No. He still travels all the time. And of course I was always busy with—"

"Work."

"Right." Her dad had his theme song, and apparently she had hers.

"I used to call him on Father's Day, but now I just send him a card. The last few years he's asked to visit me in Manhattan, but I've put him off. He's remarried now. He sent Sylvie pictures."

"So now he's making an effort." Noah's hand massaged her shoulder, as if trying to calm and comfort. "And you think it's too little, too late. Are you ever going to forgive him?"

"It's not just about what he did when I was a kid—dragging me across the country, forgetting to be my parent, using me as a show prop." Noah knew how hard her life had been growing up. She hadn't talked about it much when they'd dated, but it had come up the few holidays they'd been together. "It's that he's never tried to be anything but that guy. He knew how much all that upset me, yet he chose his music over me."

"He's made a career out of one single song?"

"That one crappy song has made him a very wealthy man." Wealthy by sensationalizing the worst time in Emma's life.

A strong gust of wind hit them as the carriage turned a corner. Noah pulled her closer. "Has he ever said he was sorry?"

"No."

He looked down, and his eyes were a little too honest, a little too intense. "Do you need that to forgive him?"

"Yes," Emma said. "I think I've been waiting a long time for that."

"And if it doesn't come?"

She tucked her head into Noah's side. "He and I go on like we always have."

"Em, your dad walked away from something incredible. I hope one day he realizes what he gave up."

Emma's pulse seized and stopped.

Because those words could just as easily apply to her. Just like her father, Emma had walked away from something incredible, chasing her own dream.

And what had she given up?

Sugar Creek.

Noah.

They would've had children by now. A house that he'd restored.

But she'd have given up her enviable career. A beautiful apartment in New York. The house she was about ready to make an offer on in Connecticut.

Yet what if she'd chosen Noah? What if she'd shoved away her fears and ran straight to the life he'd offered?

Nobody had loved her like Noah.

But would it have been enough?

9

Saturdays were for sleeping in.

Unless you had spent the last six years getting up at an hour when most college kids went to bed. Emma might've been on a sabbatical from the show, but no one had told her internal alarm clock. Fortunately, Sylvie didn't believe in snoozing away the morning either, so the two of them met at a downtown diner for breakfast. And just when Emma thought bacon would be the highlight of her day, Sylvie coaxed her into going to Crystal Bridges Museum to see a contemporary art collection titled *The Government is Watching.*

By two p.m., Emma was back home and enjoying one of her favorite rare indulgences. A nap.

At the first *thud*, Emma rolled over and burrowed deeper into the couch Frannie had loaned her from her safe room.

At the second *rrrreeeeek*, Emma opened her bleary eyes.

But when she heard footsteps on the roof, she leapt from the couch and wished she had taken Sylvie up on her offer of dueling pistols.

What in the world?

Peeling back the curtain, Emma looked out the window pane and came face to face with a metal ladder. Christmas lights littered the ground, and muffled cursing drifted to her ears. Either this was a burglar doing it the hard way or Noah Kincaid was on her roof decking out her house in lights.

After a trip to the bathroom to apply some gloss, straighten her ponytail, and rub out the pillow crease in her cheek, Emma grabbed her coat and walked outside. Dark clouds mottled the gray sky, and the wind rattled with a vicious attack on the thermometer. It had to be at least twenty degrees colder now than it had been that morning.

"You know," she said, walking out far enough to get a good look at Noah, "if Sylvie found a man tip-toeing on the top of her house, her self-designed security system would put on a laser light show big enough to zap large men and small countries."

Noah swiped his sleeve across his forehead and peered down. "I've never tiptoed in my life."

Emma smiled. "You're right. What I heard inside that house was more like angry stomping."

He angled his head with a crooked grin. "Were you sleeping in there, Miss New York City?"

She slipped her hand into a glove. "Did the pillow crease give it away?"

"I could hear you snoring from up here."

Emma laughed. "Take that back."

Noah tacked something to her chimney. "Did Sylvie wear you out today?"

"It wasn't enough that we had to go to the museum, but she had to quiz various employees on their security system. Did they have a Marx 332 or a Zettergeist M-11?" Sylvie got more than a little miffed when a manager asked if he could escort her to her car.

"Doesn't she usually drag Frannie to those things?"

"Frannie's getting back tonight from Egypt from a quick 'family reunion.' But you know what? Every one of Frannie's relatives lives in the Pacific Northwest."

The wind caught Noah's hair as he laughed. "Why don't you come up here and tell me more?"

Emma shook her head. "You know I'm scared of heights."

He peered down, those chocolate brown eyes hot on hers. "I guess some things are still the same."

Yes, like her galloping heart and the fact that the air in her head seemed to thin whenever he was around. Still the same. It had been nearly a week since their sleigh ride, and something between them had shifted.

"You don't have to decorate my house." She knew he wanted it taken care of though. Yesterday, Noah had informed her a fancy magazine on Southern life was supposed to be coming to Sugar Creek any day to check them out and write an article or two. "I scheduled someone to come out and hang the lights on Monday."

Noah chewed on his lip as he took a wire out of his pocket and applied it to a section of the lights. "Cancel it."

"Did Sylvie pay you to do this?"

"No." He walked down a slope of the roof, and Emma felt her stomach wobble. "Nobody's paying me."

Noah looked six kinds of beautiful up there, like a man battling the elements to stand atop his castle.

"I can't let you do this for free," Emma said.

"Why don't you invite me in for dinner afterward instead."

Emma didn't think she heard him right. "Can you repeat that?"

"I work. You make me something hot."

Was offering up herself the least bit appropriate? "I can do that. A hot dinner it is."

Noah gave her one of those smiles that still set her cheeks to blushing.

"What exactly is it you're working on there?" Emma backed up a few paces to see the roof better. "Is that supposed to form a word?"

"I don't have enough to spell out Scrooge, so I'm just going with E-M-M-A."

"Very funny. You know, we could simplify this and just forget the lights. I could be the bare house that symbolizes the unwillingness to roll over for the commercialism of Christmas?"

"Not in this town. We love commercialism. We roll all in it."

"Okay, well, what if—"

"Go inside, Emma." Noah drew himself up to his full height and held onto the chimney. "It's cold, you're a distraction, and you have my dinner to make."

"I see." She meant her words to sound sarcastic, but they just came out sharp. "Sorry for annoying you." With that, Emma went back inside and shuffled to the kitchen. Let him work out there in the cold. She had things to do as well. He could just entertain himself.

She pulled up her recipes on her laptop, turned on some music, and went to work. By the time Noah rang the doorbell three hours later, the sky had darkened, Emma had burned a million calories dancing to some classic Motown, and a pot of something good simmered on the stove.

Opening the door, she reminded herself to be nothing more than polite. "You probably don't want to stay. I'll pack up your food in a nice to-go bag."

Noah stretched his arm against the doorframe and leaned. "Em?"

"Yes?"

"When I said you were a distraction, I didn't mean you were annoying me."

"What did you mean?" She studied a shriveled leaf on the porch.

"That I'd rather have stood there and looked at you all day than hang sparkly things from your gutters."

Oh.

Noah slid his finger beneath her chin and lifted her gaze to his. "You gonna invite me in?"

She could think of so many things she'd like to offer. "Are you going to say yes if I do?"

His rough palm brushed against her cheek as he lowered his hand. "Try it and see."

"I think I like this new truce we have." Emma's heart did a curious pirouette.

"Just trying to be professional." He followed her into the house and sniffed appreciatively. "Chili?"

"My mom's recipe." Emma rarely had time or energy to cook, and it had been nice to putter around the kitchen today, knowing she had someone to share it with. "You're still a carnivore, right?"

"I eat anything fixed by someone else's hands." Noah pulled out a bar stool at her kitchen island as Emma ladled up some chili. She sprinkled cheese on it, added a dollop of sour cream, and handed it to him. Just the way he'd always liked it.

Emma nervously watched as he took his first bite. A trivial thing, but for some reason it mattered that he enjoyed her cooking, something she had made with her own hands.

"It's good, Em. Really good."

She wanted to be humble and contain her smile. But it slipped out anyway. "My mom used to make it on snowy days. They were some of my favorite times—waking up to a blanket of snow, school cancelled, and my mom and I having the whole day together. She'd bake, make something hot to eat, and we'd play in the snow for hours, then come back in for hot chocolate." Her eyes watered, and Emma had to look away. God, sometimes life was painful, even the good memories. Even the sweet could hurt so badly.

"You still miss her."

Emma nodded, blinking the unexpected tears away. "Something about being here in Sugar Creek—it brings so much back. The memories just come and go at their own leisure. When I was cooking today, I could feel her—my mom. I think she would've been smiling. Maybe looking over my shoulder, wishing I'd add a little more paprika."

"She'd be proud of you."

"Would she?" The words tumbled from her lips, unbidden and born from doubt. "I mean, I know career-wise, I've done okay."

"You've done more than okay. Isn't it enough?"

Something had been so off the last few years, but coming back to Sugar Creek, she felt that void even more. People in this town knew one another. There was a sense of community that had always been there, but was so pronounced now. Sugar Creek was a place where you left your screen door unlocked, you walked your children to school, and waved at your neighbor on the square. It was a town to raise a family, put down roots.

"Sometimes I do want more," Emma admitted. "It's easy to block it out back home, but not here. I think how full of life my mom was. I tend to walk around like an over-caffeinated, sleep-deprived zombie. My mom lived each day to the fullest. She was vibrant, fun, wringing every drop out of every minute."

"Like Sylvie."

"Yes. Minus the trigger finger and Kevlar bras." Emma sat on the stool next to Noah, her leg brushing his. "And what do I do? I work. And then work some more."

"And you don't like that work?"

"I do." Her words didn't sound the least bit believable. "Who wouldn't want my job?"

"You know what your mom would think about you?" Noah asked.

Emma mutely shook her head.

"Your mother would be amazed at all you've accomplished in so little time. She'd see how hard you worked in school, going to classes full time and working forty hours unpaid at the local news station. She'd be amazed at the way you've shot to the top in your field. I'm pretty sure she'd be in awe of the fact that millions of Americans have their breakfast with you every morning. She'd love your smile, your heart for Sylvie, and your brain that never quits." Noah put down his spoon and rested his hand on Emma's knee. "And she'd think you're beautiful, Emma. Just like I do."

Emma couldn't find her voice. She had to wait until the tears surrendered their chokehold on her throat. "I wish she could have gotten to know you," Emma said softly. "She'd have loved you. Your laugh, the way you work so hard, yet never hesitate to help someone."

"She sounds like a wonderful woman. And if she's anything like you, I know she was." Noah's tender words were nearly Emma's undoing.

She had to pull herself together. Crying on a man's shoulder was not something Emma did. There was something about being with Noah that just tore down her defenses and made her voice nearly every wounded thought. "Thank you for putting the lights up." Emma swiped away the moisture on her cheeks. "I'm glad this house won't be the lone eyesore on the tour."

Noah smiled. "Helping each other is what we do here."

Like a tiny pin to her balloon of expectations, Emma deflated. Was he just there for the sake of the town? Wasn't at least a small part of Noah there for her? He'd decorated her gutters, for crying out loud. Who did that? She knew he felt their connection too.

Noah's stool squawked across the wood floor as he stood. "Let's do your dishes."

"You worked all day on my house. I'll take care of it." But he was already running water over his bowl in the sink.

He placed his dish in the empty dishwasher, bumping into Emma as he turned. His hands went to her hips to steady her. "Sorry."

When his eyes locked on Emma's, *sorry* was the last thing she felt. She didn't know who stepped in first, but her hands had somehow found their way to Noah's chest. She could see his eyes darken, and suddenly Emma was twenty-one again, standing in the arms of the man who loved her, who wrote her funny poems for Valentine's Day, who took her to the drive-in and let her get the biggest popcorn there was, even though they were both college poor. Noah was still the boy who helped her hide that kitten from her apartment landlord, taking it to his place when a neighbor had ratted her out. Noah had been her first love.

And some days she wondered if he would be her last.

Rising on tip-toes, Emma leaned into Noah—

"Let's go check out your lights." He brushed her bangs from her forehead, his smile bittersweet.

Emma's balloon took a swirling nosedive to the ground.

Noah took a step back and walked toward the living room. But not before she saw that flash of regret in his eyes.

It was something.

As Noah helped Emma into her coat, she noticed his hands didn't linger. He moved fast and efficiently, then opened the front door.

In late fall in Sugar Creek, it was stumbling dark by five, but her house was lit up like a page from a winter fairy tale.

"Oh, Noah," she said breathlessly. "It's beautiful." Emma stood in the yard next to him, barely aware of the cold rushing at her from every direction. White lights outlined each line and angle of her home, with dangling snowflakes that flashed and spun as if they were falling. "You did all this for the tour." Her home looked like Christmas. Like someone who adored the holiday lived inside. "Sugar Creek is lucky to have you."

Noah looked down at Emma. "This is for you as well, Emma. I want you to see a different side of Christmas. It's not all shopping and crowds and sitting alone on the front row of your dad's concert." He wrapped his arm around her shoulder, blocking some of the wind, and pointed to her chimney. "That's the Star of Bethlehem." The heavenly beacon beamed in LED glory, like a signal to the Wise Men, to weary travelers, or those looking for their sign of hope.

And Emma wanted to hope again. She wanted to think there might be a chance she could fill the empty places in her heart. That there could be more to her life than just work. And that maybe one day Noah could be a part of it.

Emma took her gaze off the star and looked at the one who had so gallantly hung it. "Thank you."

"You're welcome." He reached out his hand and slowly lifted her hood over her head, using his fingers to tuck in the escaping strands of hair. "Emma?"

"Yes?"

"Your boss is about to make a move."

Emma couldn't move if her roof flew away. "I won't complain."

And then his hands were in her hair, her hood falling. His mouth covered hers, tentative at first, as if reacquainting itself, relearning the contours of her lips. But then the kiss deepened, both of them hungry for more. Like the house, Emma felt as if someone had lit her up with a thousand lights. No one had ever made Emma feel this combination of burn and surrender like Noah Kincaid. She strained to get closer to him, her hands sliding under his coat to explore the texture of his shirt. It still wasn't close enough.

When Noah's lips left hers, she heard her own inarticulate sound of protest. He kissed her delicate cheekbone, her forehead, finally ending at her temple, a spot of reverence and care.

Noah inhaled a ragged breath and pressed his brow to Emma's. "So you liked it?"

Emma was pretty sure she was still floating among the leafless treetops. "I more than liked it. You can kiss me any time, Mayor Kincaid."

He smiled wide. "I meant the lights."

Oh. That too.

The transformation of her house had shaken her almost as much as the kiss. Looking at those lights was like looking at a love letter written just for her.

But it was a letter Emma couldn't accept until she had said all the things she'd held onto these last ten years. "Noah"—*Spit it out. Tell him how you feel.* "When I broke our engagement—"

"I don't want to talk about it, Emma." His easy smile

dissolved like a snowflake on warm concrete as he stepped away.

"Aren't we ever going to discuss—"

"It's late. I should be going." Noah's hoarse words made her flinch. "I still have some work to do for the firm."

"But—"

"Enjoy your lights, Emma." He didn't wait for her response, but simply walked to his truck and drove away.

Emma breathed deeply, the crisp air stinging her nose. She lifted her tired eyes to the chimney where the Star of Bethlehem shined above her.

"I could use some direction, too," she whispered, her fingers pressed to her tingling lips.

On that very first Christmas centuries ago, a star had brought hope and an end to years of lonely silence.

Emma watched her own star blink and glow. "Maybe you can do the same for me."

10

She was not crying.

At least that's what Emma told herself when the doorbell rang Sunday afternoon. Blotting her damp eyes with her t-shirt, Emma muted *It's a Wonderful Life* and hustled to the door to peeked through the peephole.

Three women stood on her front porch, huddled against the tyranny of the cold. They held bags of groceries, boxes of pizza, and more Christmas decor than any of them could carry.

"Let us in!" Sylvie banged her gloved fist on the door. "I bring good tidings of drinks and pizza!"

Emma cracked open the door. "That's not all you've got." She watched her cousin Hattie nudge a large box with her foot. "What is this Christmas tree doing on my property?"

"It's *my* property," Sylvie snapped. "And I will not have any house of mine naked without a tree."

"I don't want a tree, Sylvie."

"Let me in."

"Not with all that holiday crap."

"Do you have a man in there?" Sylvie nudged past her and tromped into the house, her hens right behind her.

"There's no man."

"It wasn't going to stop us," Sylvie said. "I was just taking attendance." Her grandmother pulled at the fingers of her leopard-print gloves. "Now, back in my field days, I'd always like to know the strategic game plan. So let me lay this out for you."

Frannie nodded. "You tell her."

"We're going to eat some pizza. We're going to have a little drinkie, then we're going to decorate this barren space."

Emma knew there was just no getting out of this. The least she could do was self-medicate. "I'll get the bottle opener."

"For you, I spared no expensive. I brought very expensive wine." Sylvie held it up.

"It's in a box," Emma said.

"So are all your presents, but I'm going to toss them all out if you don't put on your happy face and get some holiday spirit."

Sylvie hadn't single-handedly stopped international terrorists on her good looks. The woman knew how to plan and maneuver, how to charm her way in and get what she wanted. Within fifteen minutes the house was rocking with music, the tree was one-fourth of the way together, and everyone had pizza on their plates.

"Give me another slice of Hawaiian," Sylvie said to Hattie. "Aloha to my tummy."

With Sylvie and Frannie neck-deep in tangled lights, Emma sat on the floor with her food.

"Can I join you?" Hattie slid a glance at the other two. "Looks like they'll be occupied for a while."

"Sure, sit."

"I bet your apartment in Manhattan is something."

"It's less than half this size, and what's *something* is the mortgage payment." Though it did have a spectacular view.

"How's the piece about Sugar Creek coming along?"

"It's just bits and pieces so far. I've talked to some folks about life before the town revitalization, and I've been interviewing people about what the new holiday events mean to them. Sugar Creek's added fifty new jobs just in the last year."

"We have Noah to thank for our growth. Even before he was mayor, he was spearheading all of that. His passion for the town is contagious, isn't it?"

It really was. Emma found herself driving by nightly and checking on all their events—not because it was her job, but because she really wanted Noah's plan to work.

"So . . . " Hattie took a bite of pizza. "Speaking of you and Noah."

"There is no me and Noah."

It was like someone dragged the needle across an old forty-five record. The whole room stopped and openly stared at Emma.

"Oh, really?" Sylvie stepped away from the mantle and sauntered to where her granddaughters sat. "Let's play a little true or false, eh? You took a carriage ride through downtown together."

"For work." Emma set her plate down. "And I'm sure I can get you a senior discount."

Hattie got in on the action. "And was he—or was he not —here last night to put lights on your house?"

"Put lights on the house?" Frannie took a sip of wine. "Is that some new slang for—"

For the love. "It means he wanted my house to be lit up for the city lights tour because *someone*"—Emma all but growled at her grandmother—"put me on the list."

"And true or false"—Hattie was enjoying this game way too much—"Noah stayed for dinner."

Frannie pushed up the bridge of her glasses. "Is dinner what you kids are calling sexy times?"

"It means Noah had chili." Frannie was reading way too many romance novels. "He strung up lights. I fixed him chili. The end." She certainly hadn't missed the way small town news traveled. "And how do you even know about that, Hattie?"

Her cousin inclined her head to a certain pixie-headed woman. "A little birdie told me."

"Does this little birdie have access to international satellites and spy cameras smaller than the head of a pin?"

Her cousin whispered behind her hand. "And a salt and pepper shaker she recently got online that picks up sound from three miles away."

Emma's gasped and pointed a shaming finger at her grandma. "Those are going in the trash."

"It was your house-warming gift."

Sylvie laughed, and soon Emma found herself joining in. Her grandmother might violate every Constitutional right to privacy, but she meant well. And it was hard to be mad at the woman who had brought a party to her house.

"Well?" Frannie perched on the arm of the couch. "We want details."

"It's nothing," Emma said. "Noah is my boss. Part of the job requires us working closely together."

Hattie rested her hand over Emma's. "Has it been tough?"

Sylvie snorted. "Oh, yeah, romantic carriage rides. Really tough."

Frannie waggled her sparse eyebrows. "Is it bringing the old magic back?"

Yes. It was bringing the magic and so much more. "He's a good man. Any woman who marries him will be . . . incredibly lucky."

"It could be you," Sylvie said.

"No." Her life was in New York. "Noah and I had our shot." And she had blown it.

"It's not too late," Hattie said. "He's available. You're available."

"We still want different things." *Didn't they?*

"Sometimes our priorities change," Frannie said. "I thought I'd stay in the CIA 'til I was holding an M-16 in one hand and my cane in the other, but one day I woke up and knew it was time to come back home and be here for my family."

Emma grinned. "Your family's all in Seattle."

She drained her wine glass. "And so far it's working out really well."

"All right." Sylvie clapped her hands for attention. "Time to get back to work. Let me review what we have so far. The tree is now assembled, the mantle lights untangled, we got some strategically placed candles, and we've established that Emma might still love Noah Kincaid."

"What?" Emma choked on her last bite of pizza. "No, I—"

"No more loafing!" Sylvie shoved a box of ornaments at Emma. "Get to decorating."

With the Christmas music singing from Hattie's phone, the ladies got to work. Though it was hard to distribute just the right amount of tinsel when her mind was on other things. Like what Sylvie had said.

Emma was *not* still in love with Noah.

She simply couldn't be.

Emma worked alongside her family, and even found herself singing along with the others to Frannie's music. Her own holidays of late had been so empty and lifeless. She wished she could freeze this moment—the laughter, the lights, the warmth in her heart at being with those she loved. This was celebrating a holiday.

"Here, Shug." Sylvie pulled Emma toward the couch some time later. "Take a look at these."

Emma slipped the lid off a red-and-gold box, her heart catching at what she saw nestled in the faded tissue paper. "Our Christmas ornaments. Where did you get these?"

"My attic. Your daddy left some of your mother's stuff the first time he lit out of Sugar Creek. I couldn't let them go to the dumpster."

Emma picked up each ornament and held it up, letting the light catch and play. They were old and inexpensive, but filled with enough love and memories to make them priceless. There was the little toy soldier her parents had bought after they'd attended the *Nutcracker* at a community theater. A seven year old Emma had slept through the entire second half. She smiled at a pair of glass angels holding golden harps. Her fingers traced the letters on a pink ornament with Emma's monogram above the words *Baby's First Christmas*.

"You made this one." Sylvie held up a popsicle-and-cotton-ball abomination. "I think you were six years old. You came back from church one Sunday with glue stuck in your hair and that piece of fine art. Your mom thought it was the most beautiful thing she'd ever seen. Said you'd surely grow up to be an artist."

Emma smiled wryly. "I grew up to flunk art in college."

"Well, your momma was an optimist." She pulled another out of the box. "Oh, this little gem was one of her favorites. You made it as well." From Sylvie's fingers dangled a small, twig-framed photo of Emma and her parents. It was the last picture of the family together before the cancer had hit. "Why don't you hang it on the tree, Shug?"

Losing her battle with tears, Emma took the thin ribbon holding the ornament, thinking of her mother's hand doing the same many years before. Walking to the blinking tree, Emma slipped it onto a narrow branch and watched the photo sway. If her mother had lived, or perhaps if her father hadn't sold out for his job, would Emma have grown up to love Christmas? What would have been different? Would she have chosen Noah over a nomadic career?

The faded image of her parents smiled at her, and Emma flicked a piece of glitter from her father's face. Maybe Noah was right, and she should let the past go. Her father's actions seemed like a desecration to Christmas and her mother's memory, but Emma definitely didn't want her own past choices held against her.

Did her father deserve that same grace?

Easier said than done.

Two bottles of wine, three empty pizza boxes, and two hours later, Emma put the star on top of her tree and stood back. The girls had surely brought Christmas. Delicate lights intertwined with burlap ribbon across the candle-lit mantle. Bing Crosby crooned about glistening tree tops, while Sylvie sang along, and Hattie and Frannie danced with golden garland wrapped about them like fine fur stoles.

This was her family.

Emma hadn't realized how fiercely she'd missed them—missed *this*—until she'd returned.

She picked up her phone, held it to get all the women in the frame, then hit record. She wanted to capture it for the possible news piece.

But mostly . . . Emma wanted to capture it for herself.

11

"Delores."

On Monday morning, Emma marched out of her office holding a red-headed doll by the hair.

Delores lowered her *People* magazine, slow as a summer sunset. "What's the problem today?"

Emma inhaled deeply, trying to breathe in calm and exhale any desire to grab the woman by her veiny throat. "I asked you to order me a backup for nativity Jesus."

Delores slid an eye to the doll held like a sub-par sacrifice. "Yeah?"

"This doll looks like a clown. It's suffocating by its own giant mop of red hair."

Delores flipped a page. "So?"

"So?" The nativity downtown was not a new tradition, nor was the occasional swiping of the holy child. Noah had commissioned a local artist to construct a new nativity, and everything had arrived but the star of the show. Emma had counted on the spare being show ready. "Baby Jesus needs to look like a sweet infant. Not like a demonic spawn on his way to the circus."

"I think you're awful closed-minded about what Jesus looks like. I thought we needed some diversity in that nativity. You want a whitey-white Jesus, you go right ahead. But when we get sued by that Al Sharpton fellow or—"

"Twenty clowns in a Fiat?"

Delores's right eye flinched. "See here—" Her voice hissed like Ursula the sea witch—"I did my job, just like you asked. You got a problem with my work, you take it up with Mr. Kincaid. Last time I checked, *he's* my boss."

Emma had interviewed drunken rap stars more pleasant than Delores.

She forced herself to unclench her fists and attempt a smile."Please call the nativity artist and check on the status of a new baby Jesus. I'm going to check on a few things downtown."

"That hot weatherman on channel five said snow's coming." Delores spun her chair until her back was to Emma. "Don't slip on any ice."

Emma was still fuming when she got out of her car. Across the street in the center of the square, two men in coats and stocking hats were unloading pieces of the nativity and putting them together. Beneath the stable, the manger sat alone, as if it knew the holy child had not been found. Following the sidewalk, Emma stepped into Tiggy's Toy Store. Run by Phillip Jasper, a retired engineer, rumored to have made his fortune in Silicon Valley, the business was now used to hold bi-weekly poker nights and occasionally sell some toys.

"Can I help you?" Phillip gnawed on an unlit cigar from his post behind the counter.

"I need a baby."

Phillip smiled. "I'm a little old and a whole lot married." He pulled the cigar from his lips. "Though I could be talked into sharing a double scoop at the ice cream joint three doors down."

"I meant a doll. The nativity has suffered a small setback, and Jesus won't be arriving until next week."

"The Wise Men are really gonna be ticked at that. All right, let's find what you need."

Five minutes later Emma emerged from the store with a suitable doll and an invitation to Texas Hold 'Em. Her toes pinched in her black patent heels as she walked to the nativity, snow lightly spitting. The workers were now nowhere to be seen, so she made her way to the manger and gently laid the baby inside.

"Emma?"

Her hands froze on the doll, and she closed her eyes for a sobering beat before turning to face the one standing behind her.

"Dad."

Edward Casey, songwriter and singer of "A Christmas Broken Heart," of the apprehensive face, salt-and-pepper hair, and silver wedding band, looked as out of place on that town square as he was in Emma's life.

"What are you doing here?" Emma had too many worlds colliding. "I thought this was your busiest time."

"It is. I, um, I'm performing at some casinos over the Oklahoma line, and I thought I'd spend some time in Sugar Creek. My wife and I are staying at the cabins out east of town. It's a little bit of a drive, but I couldn't pass it up." He smiled hesitantly. "Did you get my wedding announcement I sent you?"

"I did." Her brain sputtered for words to fill the space. "Did you get my . . . Crock-Pot?"

"Yes. Cheryl said it was a real nice one. Had a timer and everything, right?"

This was the conversation of two people who were strangers. Instead of father and child.

"Sugar Creek's really changed huh?" Her father glanced around appreciatively, snow sticking to his coat. "It's homey, isn't it?"

"Yes, it is." On that they could agree. "I should go. I need to get back to work."

"You're working here?"

"Just for the rest of the month." Emma felt childishly defensive over her job hiatus. "I'm helping with the town Christmas preparations while I take some time off from the show."

"Yeah, I saw you on TV. I guess people get a little upset when you bash a holiday."

Emma's voice went flat. "For some reason, I've just never felt that warm flow of the season."

"Well." Her father cleared his throat. "I'll be here for most of the month. Believe it or not, I'm taking the week before Christmas off. My wife kind of put her foot down."

His *wife*.

She knew her father had remarried, but it hurt, hearing it from his lips and getting confirmation the woman was a real person.

"You better get off the streets." Her father moved as if to hug her, but patted her shoulder instead. "It's really starting to come down. I hope to see you around."

Emma didn't know how long she stood there. Long after her father ambled away, as if he'd tossed a bomb and hadn't bothered to look back at the destruction. He never had.

The damp snow finally penetrated her coat, and Emma pulled herself from her dark, swirling thoughts. A thin veil of flakes covered the ground all around her, her shoulders, even the tips of her hair. She had been too gobsmacked by running into her father to even notice.

The cold metal of the car door handle bit into Emma's skin as she got in and drove back to city hall on autopilot. Had she stopped at the four-way? Had she slowed down at that speed trap on Davis? Seeing her dad in Sugar Creek was like watching your favorite TV show, only to see a character from a different network walking on. Her dad simply wasn't in her cast; he didn't belong in her scenes.

The city administration building was practically empty when Emma stepped inside.

Delores lifted her head long enough to glower. "Have you seen your hair?"

Emma didn't know what compelled her, but her legs moved almost of their own will right to Noah's office. She didn't bother to knock, just stumbled in and shut the door behind her.

Noah sat behind his desk, phone held to his ear. He took one look at Emma and stood. "Bob, I'll call you back. Something important just came up." He tossed the phone on the desk. "Emma, what's wrong?"

Without a single thought to decorum, Emma rushed to Noah, hugged him fiercely, and just held on.

Noah's arms immediately wrapped around her. "Are you okay?" His hand stroked down the back of her head.

"I'm fine." She wasn't an emotional person. To be a success in her career, Emma had to have a PhD in *not* reacting, not giving into feelings. But today . . . it had just been too much.

"Want to tell me what happened? Did Delores snap at you again?"

She burrowed into his warmth and shook her head. "I was downtown. I saw my dad."

His body stilled. "He's here?"

Emma attempted to pull away, but Noah kept her in place, pressed to him, her cheek against his heart. "He's performing at some casinos in Oklahoma. He'll be here through Christmas."

"I'm sorry."

There came a point in every meltdown when reason kicked in. Emma knew she was acting ridiculous. She had to pull it together, nice as it was right in this spot. "I'm sorry. I shouldn't have barged into your office and thrown myself at you." Emma sniffed and cursed the obnoxious tears that fell. "It just threw me, you know?"

"He should've called you."

"He's married." She realized her hands were all but petting the back of Noah's sweater and made herself stop. "I knew he was married, but I saw his wedding ring, and he mentioned his wife like . . . like it was no big deal. It was as if I were talking to a distant uncle, someone I used to know." She looked up at Noah. "He's not my mother's husband anymore."

"But in some ways, he'll always be." He brushed a wet strand of hair from her cheek, his fingers a warm arc across her skin. "Your father getting remarried doesn't negate his time with your mother. I'm sure he loved her."

"Loved her so much he cashed in on her death?" Ugh, she sounded like she was twelve! She wasn't this hurt little girl anymore. She was an adult; a mature, level-headed adult. One look at her father, and she was right back to that angry fourteen year old who had called her grandmother and said, "Enough."

But she couldn't stand there and whine all over Noah.

"I'm sorry." Emma pushed away from him, her cheeks rosy with embarrassment. "You smell nice by the way." *Oh, my gosh.* This is what the peaks of stress did to her—made her completely lose her filter. *I hate Christmas, America! You smell nice! I want you to kiss me until I think of nothing but you!*

"Oh, geez!" Emma threw out her hands, fending off Noah's advance. "Don't come near me." She was liable to say anything! "I didn't mean to fall apart." She slowly retreated toward the door. "It was such a shock to see my dad, and it started snowing kind of crazy, not that I even noticed, and now my hair's a mess, and I knew you would understand, but I didn't mean to get all weird and teary and handsy and sniffy and—"

"Emma?" Noah walked toward her.

"Yes?"

"I'm glad you came to me." His eyes never wavered from hers. "Once upon a time you told me everything."

She sighed. "I did, didn't I?" *That* had to have been ten kinds of fun. "You poor, poor man."

"I've missed it." His next words had her grabbing the door for support. "I've missed you."

Clearly the man did not know that Emma's self-control was currently as strong as a toothpick, as he closed the distance between them and put his hand over hers on the doorknob. She wanted so badly to trace the contours of his face with her hand, to feel that faint stubble tickle her fingers, to slip her arms around his waist and kiss him until he had forgotten she was the girl who had tossed his heart in the dirt and walked away.

"Do you remember what we'd do when you got upset over your dad in the college days?" he asked quietly.

Noah was so close, she could barely remember her own name. "You . . . " *Focus, Emma.* "You would take me to the student union, and we'd split a cheeseburger and fries."

"There's a diner on the square that has the best shakes in town. How about I buy, and you talk?"

Her lips eased into a slow smile. "Are you asking me out?"

He tugged on her scarf until each end was even. "Consider it a dairy-fueled counseling session."

"The weather's getting pretty bad out there. Are you sure you want to go?"

"We've still got a few hours before the town shuts down."

Emma hoisted her purse strap on her shoulder and looked into his smiling eyes. "I used to thank you for the shake and fries with a big make out session."

Noah gently nudged her out the door and turned out the lights. "Some parts of history are definitely worth revisiting."

12

"Sugar Creek needed Jesus."

At least that's what Mrs. Carson had said when she'd called Emma the next evening.

"Honey, somebody has stolen baby Jesus right out of that manger."

"Mrs. Carson, there's at least six inches of snow on the ground." From her warm spot on the couch, Emma watched the lights twinkle on the Christmas tree. "What are you doing checking on the nativity?"

"I walked by there on my way to see about my mother. I'm a block away, and I said to myself, *I better peek in on Jesus.* I didn't want our Lord and Savior covered in frozen precipitation. But you know what? Our Lord and Savior wasn't even there."

"Maybe someone took him inside for some hot chocolate."

"No, they didn't."

"He's probably at the corner bar."

"Religious jokes are never in good taste."

Mrs. Carson did not seem to have the joy deep down in her heart.

"If that fancy magazine is in town," she said, "we'll never be able to hold our heads up. You cannot have a nativity without the baby Jesus. The liberals will think we've joined them on the dark side."

Now it was a Republican manger? "Look, all I have as a replacement is a girl doll with a scary red wig. Her hair probably won't even fit in the manger."

"That'll do. Just cover up her head. Pastor Thomas's church will get riled up if they think you're trying to make a statement about the Lord's gender. The All Souls Church on Davis would probably write you a thank you note."

"Good bye, Mrs. Carson."

"Are you going to take care of this?"

Her rental car was a tin can on wheels. It sure didn't have four-wheel drive. "It's pretty slick out there. And very cold."

"I see." Emma could hear a pen tapping on the other end. "Has the mayor told you how much is riding on our town's success with this Christmas business?"

It truly was a business. Where was it not? "I believe he's mentioned it."

"It's important. Every single detail is so very important. Lots of folks here saw you on the television. They didn't think you should be in charge of our Christmas activities, but Noah assured us you could do it."

The woman knew just the right button to push.

The big flashing one that said NOAH.

She had promised Noah she would give Sugar Creek Christmas. Told him she'd work her butt off. She knew he was probably still expecting her to fail, and she was not going to be foiled by a baby doll. If that magazine did stop by the nativity, they were going to see something in that manger if she had to sleep in it herself.

"Consider it taken care of," Emma said.

Emma grabbed her purse, her indignant attitude, one ugly baby doll, and got in her car. Snow already frosted the ground, the streets, and the housetops. Early that morning, the city's offices and schools had announced their closures, so Emma had spent the entire day in her yoga pants and sweatshirt working on her story for *Sunrise News* from the couch. The roads in her part of town were curvy at best, but surely if she took it really slow, she would be fine.

And that's what she told herself as her car slid all the way down Harrison. Emma prayed to that stolen baby Jesus as her car fish-tailed onto Forrest Street. She clutched the steering wheel with both hands, her grip locked, her jaw set, her eyes trained on the road. But it was so hard to see. Her windshield wipers were a joke, barely scraping a clear spot to look out of. The radio seemed much too loud, so Emma shut it off. She could not concentrate with Beyonce riding along.

Emma saw the small hill on the next road and knew she had to give the car some gas or she'd never make it up.

God, help me.

She pressed the pedal, heard the engine rev, and the little sedan pushed through the snow and climbed its way up.

Then spun out before she got to the top.

"No, no. Come on. You can make it." Emma gave it more gas, but the tires just whirled in place. "This cannot be happening. Just a bit further." But one more tap on the gas was too much. The car swerved and wiggled. Backward.

Emma mashed her foot on the brake. She wilted against the steering wheel when the car obeyed and froze in place.

Yet it still clung to the hill. On her right was a ditch. On her left was a ravine. It might be a ditch. She was a little unclear when one became the other, but what she did know was that if a car went into the drop-off on the left, it would swallow the vehicle whole. And that would hurt just a tiny bit.

"Just going to ease up on the brake," she coached herself, "and drive this thing in reverse"

As if tugged by an invisible string, the car turned left. Emma pulled on the steering wheel, but the tires would not straighten.

She tried again.

In her side mirror, the ravine loomed perilously close.

Emma laid on the brake again.

But the brakes gave up.

Emma yanked on the wheel and yelled out a prayer.

The little red rental finally cooperated, and to the right it went.

Tail-first into the ditch.

Her head bounced against the seat and ricocheted off her side window at the abrupt stop. Her breath coming in pants, Emma did a mental scan of her quaking body and found not one bone protesting. Though her smarting head would later require some aspirin. And ice cream. When she got out of this mess and safely back home, she would definitely be having ice cream. Perhaps a whole gallon.

But for now, she and the car were in a bit of a predicament.

It could be worse, Emma quickly reminded herself.

The running car shook and sputtered, gave one great shudder, and died.

"Are you kidding me?" Her shaking fingers turned the key, but the ignition merely clicked.

Her gas gauge pointed right to the red letter E.

E for empty.

E for *everything is wrong*!

Reaching into her purse, Emma felt for her phone. She found two used tissues, a Snickers wrapper, five lip glosses, and a useless pair of sunglasses. Only total idiots and weirdos went into this kind of weather without a phone!

The wind and snow slapped at the windows, and it was mere minutes before the frigid temperatures leaked into the car, turning it into an icebox. She peered in the backseat for her coat, but found nothing but a flimsy running jacket.

"I've got to get out of here and find help." Her breath puffed from her lips. "I don't want Sylvie to find my body tomorrow, frozen like a fish stick." Good heavens, she was already talking to herself. Probably the first sign of hypothermia.

Straining to open the driver's side door, Emma was shocked by a whoosh of brutal air and the thud of the door hitting the bank. Crawling out of that tiny opening would be impossible. Flinging off her seatbelt, she grabbed the doll and climbed over the console and opened the passenger door. It would be a small drop, but she had taken five years of gymnastics as a child. Emma could dismount with the best of them. In third grade she'd gotten the junior Olympic—

She landed butt-first in a mound of snow and mud. Emma blinked against the sleet snapping against her skin and pushed herself to her feet. Up the hill was a series of houses. And that darn nativity.

The road was glazed as an ice rink, so with doll under her arm, Emma trudged through the ditch and climbed to the top. She spied what used to be her junior English teacher's house and crossed through her yard.

Nobody was home.

Fine. There were lights on in the house across the street. She'd try them.

So cold. Her shivering lips tasted ice.

Stepping onto the street, Emma stayed upright an entire thirty seconds before her feet betrayed her and went two different directions. The fall sent her to her knees on the grass. Just in time to see headlights coming her way.

A truck stopped and Noah rolled down his window. "What in the heck are you doing?"

Her hair clung to her face in frozen clumps. "Making social calls. What does it look like I'm doing?"

"Crawling on the ground with some kid's doll." He hopped out of the truck and ran to her as if he were so athletic, so stealthy, he was immune to the ice. "Hang on. I've got you." Noah slipped his arm around Emma and pulled her to him. "You look like a drowned rat."

With numb fingers, she flicked a blob of mud from her sweatshirt. "Sometime you should Google 'ways to compliment the ladies.'"

"Where's your car?"

"In a ditch." She pointed the opposite direction. "Down the hill a ways." Taking a little siesta.

"Get in the truck." Noah shucked out of his wool coat and draped it across Emma's shoulders. He assisted her into his in truck, reaching across her body to pull out the seatbelt.

"Hey, watch the hands." She slapped them away. "I can do that."

His shoulder brushed against her cheek. "Would you just accept some help?" Noah was still shaking his head when he got in and put the truck in drive.

"Thanks for picking me up," Emma said.

Noah cut her a sharp look. "You want to tell me what you were doing out here?"

"Fixing the nativity. Someone stole Jesus."

He flexed his hands on the steering wheel. "Sylvie is going to kill you."

"If Sylvie had been me, she would've done the same." Or arranged for a drone delivery. "I need you to take me to the nativity."

"The manger can wait. You could've been hurt on these roads. It only takes fifteen minutes of ice before they're dangerous, Emma."

Of course she knew this. Everyone who lived in the county knew it could go from zero to a Polar Slip 'N Slide in a matter of minutes. "Please drive me to the nativity." She attempted to bat her eyes at Noah, but her lashes just stuck together. "I've come this far."

Noah gave her a look that clearly communicated his doubts about Emma's mental faculties, but he steered the truck in that direction. The nativity soon came into view, the great star suspended from a tree and illuminating the scene.

He parked the truck and held out a hand. "Let me have it."

"It's not your baby."

"Thank God for that."

Emma hopped out, but wasn't surprised to hear his footsteps crunching behind her, along with some muttering that didn't sound too Christmassy.

"That is one ugly doll," he said.

"Well, don't tell the Presbyterians."

"What?"

"Nothing." She swiped at her drippy nose and stopped to dump some snow from her shoe. "But I'm pretty sure they serve sour grapes for communion at Mrs. Carson's church."

"Em, I'll take that for you." He reached for the doll.

"Get back! This is my job. I will tend the manger . . . and watch the flock by night." Delirium was clearly setting in. The cold had passed through her wet yoga pants and gone right to her bones. Even her underwear was wet. She'd walked miles and miles on the snowy sidewalks of New York, but never in her life had she endured frozen knickers.

On stiffened legs, Emma approached the nativity nestled in the middle of the town square. With a numb hand, she swiped the melted flakes from her face like a windshield wiper. Speakers piped holiday carols, and she paused long enough to slip her arms into Noah's coat and gaze at the scene around her.

God had dropped her in a storybook village.

Every good citizen of Sugar Creek was bundled inside their toasty homes, and the world was a quiet hush of falling snow and soft, lilting music. Lights haloed the nativity, with the Wise Men offering gifts, Mary staring at the manger in wonder, and Joseph with his head bowed in prayer.

"A local artist from Eureka Springs carved and painted every piece." Noah came up behind Emma as they stopped before the holy family.

"It's . . . beautiful."

Noah's hands rested on her shoulders and lightly squeezed. "Very beautiful."

"Oh, the cards. Still a tradition, huh?" She walked to the manger and picked up one of hundreds littering the hay. Even though the nativity had changed, the littering of prayers had not. Every season, folks would write prayers on cards and leave them at the nativity until they formed a floor for the manger.

Dear Jesus, she read.

It's been a tough year. I'm praying for healing for my husband. He has stage three cancer . . .

Emma sent up a silent prayer for the person and picked up another card.

God, I don't pray that much, but I need your help. I've been out of work for a whole year and . . .

She read three more before the cold and sorrow were too much. "Such desperate pleas."

Noah hugged her shivering body to his and ran his hands up and down her back. "I guess you know something about desperate Christmas prayers."

She closed her eyes and rested her head on his dampened shirt. "There's something about the season that makes us think anything is possible. And we will ourselves to hope . . . just one more time. Believing—" She couldn't even finish her thought. There was no sense in revisiting those dark memories, when she'd spent all Christmas Eve on her knees, begging God to heal her mom. But God had had other ideas, and her beloved mother had been gone by morning. And in so many ways, so had her dad.

Noah kissed the top of her soggy head. "No matter what happens, your hope is never wasted."

She blinked back tears. "I wish I could scoop up all those cards and grant every one of their wishes."

"It's not your job, Emma." Noah hugged her closer. "It never was."

13

From the warmth of the dark cab, Noah looked at her car with its front end sticking up like it wanted to wave howdy-do. Body tense, he set his jaw and slowly turned his head to Emma. "You were in a ditch."

She graced him with a gentle smile. "I did tell you that part."

"Do you see the other side of this road?" His voice vibrated dangerously low. "You could've killed yourself."

"Not likely." She employed Smile Number Seven, the one reserved for celebrities ready to storm off the set. "There's lots of snow. Look how plush it is."

Noah's eyes narrowed, and she pried his right hand from the steering wheel and held it. "I'm okay, Noah. It was a stupid idea, but I don't want any of the Christmas plans to derail. If that magazine had—"

"Forget the magazine." He punched the button for her heated seat and resumed their drive. "The doll could've waited 'til the roads cleared. The least you could've done was call me."

"I didn't want to bother you."

"Did you think I wouldn't have helped you?" He turned onto Harrison, the street lights strangely dark.

"Come on," she said quietly. "It's just in the last week you've even let yourself talk to me." She regretfully let his hand go, only to for him to grab hers right back.

"You're freezing." He placed her hand on his thigh and briskly ran his fingers across her skin. "Why didn't you call when you hit the ditch?"

"Left my phone at home."

The words he said under his breath would've curled Christmas ribbon.

The ice and snow intensified, battling one another for dominance as they fell onto the truck. Noah's wiper blades screeched in protest to a hard night's work against the frozen elements. The feeling began to return to Emma's limbs, and though she was chilled to the core, a different sort of warmth unfurled at the feel of Noah's skin on hers.

He blew out a resigned sigh. "You're doing a good job, Emma."

"Oh." She hadn't expected that. "Thank you."

"But the manger could've waited."

"I wasn't going to be able to sleep if I didn't fix it." And all those notes scattered around it just proved how much that nativity meant to the town.

"You about slept in the ditch." Not only did Noah's gruff tone not intimidate her, it made her smile.

"I was about to get help when you showed up. Why were *you* out, by the way?"

"Took some firewood to your grandma. She tried calling you while I was there. She was worried."

"Like she doesn't have a tracking device on all her grandchildren."

"I called her when I saw you sprawled in the snow. She

can rest easy now. But if you get pneumonia, she'll probably kill the both of us." He gave her hand a squeeze. "Silently and without leaving evidence."

Emma's grin slipped. "You missed my driveway."

Noah pulled into his own driveway and locked those electric eyes on Emma. "You're spending the night with me."

Emma's breath stalled. "I don't think so."

Ignoring that, Noah shut off the truck, grabbed a flashlight beneath his seat, and seconds later opened her door. "The electricity's out in the whole neighborhood. Did you get your chimney cleaned?"

Shoot. "I did think about it."

"Then you have no heat."

Heat was the one thing she wanted. Well, and if she were honest with herself, maybe a little more cuddle time with Noah. "I can just bundle up. I'll be fine."

"I'm not having your frozen carcass on my conscience."

"Gosh, I love it when you talk sexy."

"Come on. I've already promised Sylvie I'd take care of you." Noah gently put his hand under her arm. "Let's go, babe."

Babe. He used to call her that all the time. Holy hand warmers, she had missed it.

With his arm covering her like a wing of protection against the relentless snow, Noah led her inside his darkened home. He pulled a shivering Emma through his foyer, past the living room with a crackling fire, and toward his staircase.

"Wait, what are you doing?"

"Taking you to my bedroom."

She tried to read his face in the faint glow of his flashlight. "Noah?"

Noah laughed quietly and pushed a strand of wet hair from her cheek. “You need to change into some dry clothes.”

“I have clothes at my house.”

He tilted his head and regarded her, looking more than a little charming. “Afraid you can’t trust yourself with me in my bedroom?”

“Of course not.” Well, maybe a little. Okay, a lot. Like a whole, whole lot.

Noah’s mouth curved. “We’ll get your clothes tomorrow.” He shined the light on the staircase and motioned for her to lead the way. “After you cook me breakfast.”

Oh, now that was funny. “Dream on.”

“You owe me, Sutton,” he said, using her television last name. Legally she still carried the last name of Casey, but when she’d gotten her first television gig, she’d used her mother’s maiden name.

It was hard to navigate stairs when your feet were blocks of ice. Emma stumbled halfway up, but strong hands were there to steady her. “Okay, if the power’s back on, I owe you breakfast.”

They reached the landing, and Noah guided her to the master suite. The room was cast in shadows, but she could see it had been renovated. A king-sized bed sat against the far wall, and thick crown molding framed the entire space. Emma wondered if he’d remodeled it himself or if he’d had a woman’s input. She didn’t want to think about that.

Noah disappeared into a walk-in closet, only to return a moment later, filling her hands with a pile of clothes as well as the flashlight. “Go take a hot shower.” He pointed to the door on the opposite wall. “I’ll have the fire waiting for you downstairs.”

A half hour later, Emma padded into the living room. The snow tapped against the fogged window, but Noah stood at the fireplace and stoked the coals, as if determined to battle the cold away from them. The flames crackled and hissed a melodic, soothing's Emma's weary heart.

"I love a good fire." Emma settled onto the couch, tucking her legs beneath her.

Noah smiled as he took in her attire. "Nice outfit."

"They're a little roomy." Emma wore a pair of his sweats, the waistband cinched, a thermal shirt, and a University of Arkansas hoodie. She leaned her nose into her shoulder. "I smell like you." She wished she could bottle up that scent and pull it out on days when she ached with missing him.

Noah studied her in his sweatshirt, and his lips curved into a smile. "You feeling warmer?"

Oh, was she.

Emma burrowed deeper into the couch. "I remember sitting in front of the fire with my parents on Christmas Eve."

The firelight cast wild shadows on the floor as Noah added more wood to the flames, then moved toward her. "So your Christmases weren't all bad."

She shook her head, the ends of her slightly-damp hair brushing against her neck. "We'd eat cookies and watch movies. My plans were always to wait out Santa Claus, but I'd fall asleep watching the flames, only to wake up Christmas morning in my own bed."

Noah lifted a blanket from the end of the leather couch and spread it over Emma, his hands sliding over her as he tucked her in. "Those are the memories we hold on to. The good ones."

He was right. But easier said than done. "I always thought if I had children, I'd make Christmas a big deal like my mom did. We'd bake fudge, trim the tree, read the Christmas story. Have some traditions."

"Still lots of time for that."

"Children don't really fit into my life at the news desk right now. I travel a lot. Have long hours."

He stared down at Emma. "Is that what you want?"

A year ago, she wouldn't have even thought about her answer. She had worked her butt off to get where she was, and the lead anchor chair was right within her reach. Just a few more years, just a few more breakout stories.

Yet the thought of returning made her as frozen inside as the snow covering the city.

"My career's been incredibly good to me," she said finally. "Well, minus one very dramatic firing."

"But is it still what you want?" Noah was not going to let that question go. "Does it make you happy?"

"No," she said honestly. "But does anyone's job? As kids, we have this fantasy that we'll grow up to be something that's fun, that fuels a passion. But so few people get that."

"I have that. I enjoy the law practice."

"And you're like a kid in a candy store with all the city planning."

"If I didn't like the work, I wouldn't do it."

"It's not that easy. I have a degree and a lot of years invested in this career. And if I keep my nose out of trouble, I'm on the path that leads right to the lead anchor seat."

"What would you be if you weren't on the show?"

Emma hadn't ever let herself think about alternatives. She'd just trudged on, as if the answer to her occupational melancholy had simply been *more work*. "I don't know." She ran her hand over the fleecy blanket and smiled. "Don't tell anyone, but I'm kind of enjoying the marketing job, even if it is organizing events for a difficult holiday."

"You're good at it," Noah said. "Melissa's husband told me yesterday they're not sure she'll return to work. Apparently the thought of leaving her baby with a sitter has her crying on a daily basis." He paused and watched Emma closely. "Know anyone who would want the job?"

The man was all temptation tonight. "It's not me, Noah," Emma said quietly. "I have my eye on a goal in New York, and I've got to see it through."

"Even if you're miserable?"

The wind howled and rattled the windows, and Emma shivered. She pulled the blanket to her chin and closed her eyes, leaving his question unanswered. "I don't think I'm ever going to get warm again."

The couch sank as Noah sat down, his thigh brushing hers. "Come here." He pulled her to him and shifted them both until they were lying down, his arms holding her tight like a cherished present. He rested his chin on her head and absently stroked her blanket-covered arm. "Sylvie called while you were in the shower. She says to stay put."

Emma smiled languidly. "I'm too tired to argue."

"I guess you can add this to your Christmas memory collection."

Emma twisted until she faced him. "Noah?" She slipped her hand from the blanket and brushed it across his stubbled cheek. "I think I love this memory already."

He lowered his head, let his lips hover over hers. "This is probably not a good idea."

There was too much space between them. Emma pulled his head to hers. "Let me know when you get a better one." She kissed him with all the Thankful-Damsel-in-a-Ditch energy that pulsed through her veins. It had been ten years since they'd been together. Too long to go without this man's hands on her. He rolled her beneath him and took control. His lips teased and soothed, reminding her of what it felt like to be his, to be cherished, adored. Her fingers threaded through his hair, as Noah changed the angle and intensity, using lips, teeth, and tongue.

Noah raised his head just enough to look at Emma, stroking her face. His eyes held the same tenderness she had seen so many years before.

And Emma knew she was utterly lost.

She knew the feeling the second it pinged in her heart—that lonely spot only he'd ever reached. That heart spiraled and tilted like a snowflake in a storm, unable to do anything but fall. She had loved Noah once. It was right there again, tapping at the frosty window-pane, begging her to let it in.

Emma drifted her hands down Noah's strong back, needing to draw closer as he lowered his lips once more. He rained feathery kisses across her cheek, taking a little detour to the sensitive flesh of her neck, only to slide back up to match his lips to hers again.

"Still cold?" With a smile, he pressed his forehead to hers, his breathing ragged, his heart beating steadily against her palm.

"Definitely warming up." Her hand traced the contour of his cheek. "You run a full-service rescue operation."

Turning on his side, Noah pulled her to him. The two watched the flames shimmy in the fireplace, his hand making lazy strokes down her arm. A million thoughts flitted through Emma's mind. Was tonight just an anomaly? Would she return to work in city hall, only to find her cold, aloof boss had returned? What if this was nothing more than a moment of weakness for him? A trip back in time?

"I can hear the gears turning in your head." His voice rumbled against her. "Whatever it is you're worrying over, don't."

"Are we going to talk about what just happened?"

He kissed the top of her head. "Not tonight."

She didn't know why she was disappointed. It wasn't like she had any idea what to say.

They'd kissed.

It probably meant nothing to him. He probably kissed women all the time.

Now that was just a depressing thought.

Emma squeezed her eyes shut against the image in her head. She didn't want to think of Noah with anyone else.

Which bothered her even more.

He wasn't hers. And she'd be leaving next month.

Emma didn't know how long she lay there brooding, but she knew she wouldn't be able to sleep until she gave Noah the words on her heart. She whispered his name and gave his arm a small shake.

"What?" He tightened his hold and breathed deeply.

"I'm sorry."

He softly squeezed her hand. "I know."

"I'm not talking about driving into a ditch."

Noah ran his hand over her hair. "I know, Em."

Somehow it was easier to get it all out with him holding her close—yet not looking into his face. "I . . . I was afraid of the life you wanted."

Her words went without comment long enough that she thought maybe he had fallen asleep.

Until finally she heard his voice.

"I guess I was afraid of your dream too," Noah said.

"I shouldn't have just walked out." Emma hated the way the day replayed in her mind. "I handled it so badly, and if I could go back, I would. I'd change it. I'm sorry I hurt you." The fire snapped and popped, and she imagined her old wounds going up in the smoke that filled the chimney and escaped into the night sky. "I need you to forgive me, Noah. I can't keep going on like this. Maybe

God led me to Sugar Creek just to tell you one last time how sorry I am."

His voice whispered near her ear. "I forgive you."

A weight of a hundred Christmas trees lifted from Emma's heart. She'd been carrying that guilt for so long. Parts of it would always stay with her, tucked in her mind like a splinter she couldn't see. Maybe one day she'd be able to forgive herself and let it completely go. For now, she had the most important thing. Noah's absolution.

"Thank you." She nestled into the crook of his arm, placed a reverent kiss against his skin, and breathed him in. "Thank you."

Emma fell asleep in Noah's arms.

She was warm. She was safe.

She was still in love.

14

Two nights later, nearly all traces of snow had disappeared, as if the wintery precipitation had packed up its every belonging and left in a snit, offended at the arrival of the sun.

Standing before the bathroom mirror, Emma applied Vixen Violet lipstick to her lips and blotted them with a tissue. Her stomach was full of a protein bar and butterflies, neither one particularly satisfying. In just a few hours, the town would put on their coats and gloves and pile onto the lawn of the square for the tree lighting ceremony. Emma had reviewed every single detail at least a dozen times, but she still felt as nervous as the time she'd interviewed her first royal. Tonight's event was the bow on top of a very big, strategically planned package.

Her doorbell rang, and Emma frowned. She did not have time for visitors.

In her camel-colored dress pants, white cashmere sweater, and leather stiletto boots, Emma made her way downstairs and opened the door.

She smiled at the sight of her guest. "Noah."

He stood on her front porch, a bouquet of hot pink roses in his hand. "I was in the neighborhood." He leaned in for a long, lingering kiss. "Thought you might want a ride."

Emma held the flowers between them and sniffed. "You're such a gentleman to come all this way."

"Anything for you." He nudged her inside and shut the door behind them.

"Thank you for the roses. They're—"

Noah pulled her to him and silenced her with another kiss, tossing the flowers in a nearby camping chair.

"I should put those in water."

Though Emma was struggling to recall where her kitchen even was.

"It can wait." His lips settled on the soft spot beneath her ear as he pressed her back to the door.

"They might wilt."

"I'll buy you more."

Emma wanted to stay like this forever—in Noah's arms, his lips on hers, his body close. With just one touch from him, she felt safe, cherished, even loved.

But what did he feel about her? Besides the obvious attraction, did Noah think about Emma as much as she did of him? Did thoughts of her interrupt his workday and dominate his nights? She wondered if Noah could he falling for her or if she were merely a holiday fling.

"We could stay here." Noah's soft lips whispered against hers. He tasted like heaven and temptation, but inside her head Emma heard the ticking of the clock, counting down her days left in Sugar Creek.

"I kind of think the mayor has to be at the city tree lighting." Emma rested her head against Noah's chest, loving the sound of his racing heart against her ear.

"So I need a date for the Christmas gala," Noah said.

"Oh." Emma smiled. "Got anyone in mind?"

"Delores has been dropping hints."

She laughed. "I'm willing to fight her for you." Emma pressed a quick kiss to Noah's chin. "I just confirmed the band's airfare yesterday."

Noah hugged her closely. "I think this will be our best gala yet."

It as also the last event of the holiday season, just a few days before Christmas.

Then Emma would be gone.

Noah and Emma walked around the square, putting the final touches on each aspect of the event. The weather had come through, thankfully. It was a chilly forty-five degrees, but the sky was clear and there wouldn't be precip for days.

"Everything looks great," Emma said as Noah walked with her across the crispy, dried lawn. "You've done a fabulous job."

He trailed a knuckle down her cheek. "I couldn't have done it without you."

Emma laughed. "I'm sure you would've found a way."

"Let me rephrase that, I wouldn't have *wanted* to have done this without you."

Her heart soared like the fireworks that would later fly over the creek. "I didn't expect to enjoy all this Christmas planning," Emma admitted. "But I have. I've loved my time here."

Noah reached for Emma's hand, meshing their fingers. "Then don't go back."

"I . . .it's tempting. What I do is interesting, but it's not the fulfilling career I thought it would be."

"Even meeting all those famous people. You've become a celebrity yourself."

But it *wasn't* enough. "Maybe I'm just burned out. It could pass."

"And what if it doesn't?" Noah frowned. "Do you really want to spend a few more decades in a job that makes you miserable?"

Like it was that easy—to just quit and leave a lucrative television career behind. "What else would I do? My resume is just a series of news jobs."

"And now you can add marketing director—city event planner."

Emma smiled at a passerby. "Sometimes I imagine myself quitting my job and trying something new. But that fantasy never ends well."

"Melissa put in her notice today." Noah's eyes were steady on Emma's. "It seems I have a job opening."

"Mayor Kincaid!" The man who had the honor of turning on the Christmas tree lights waved from across the lawn, saving her from a response.

"I need to take care of some things and go meet everyone on stage." Noah waved and returned his attention back to Emma. "Are you sure I can't talk you into joining me up there? I'd like the town to see the woman behind so much of our Christmas success."

"That's really sweet, but my answer is still no. I'm enjoying being out of the spotlight."

Noah led Emma to an empty seat on the front row, right next to Delores.

"I'm proud of you," he said to Emma. "Sugar Creek is better with you here." Then in front of God, country, and one giant Christmas tree, Noah kissed her. With a playful wink, he walked away.

And Emma all but collapsed into her chair.

Beside her, Delores gave a disdainful snort. "Is that in your job description? He's never kissed me like that."

Emma watched Noah approach the stage as she leaned toward his receptionist. "It was in my contract."

Half an hour later, the moon shone on Sugar Creek and the thousands of folks who had gathered for the celebration. Noah welcomed everyone, giving props to all who had been involved in bringing Christmas to the town, from various civic organizations to individuals. When he thanked Emma, the entire crowd had clapped and cheered. It would be another memory to pull out on the hard days back in Manhattan.

As Noah continued to speak eloquently about the community of Sugar Creek and the joy of the season, Emma joined the volunteers to pass out candles to everyone there.

After Noah stepped down, accompanied by a standing ovation, the Sugar Creek children's choir assembled on stage.

"They were specifically asked not to sing any songs by your father," Noah whispered as he returned to Emma's side.

She cuddled into the arm he offered and kissed his cheek. "Thank you."

As the children sang, many of the onlookers joined in while they began the chain of lighting their candles.

Next, a city council member introduced their honorary tree-lighter, a twenty six-year old Army veteran who had returned from Afghanistan only months ago with new medals on his uniform, but without his right leg and two of his closest friends.

The soldier didn't leave a dry eye as he thanked the

community for their support and expressed gratitude for being home—alive—with his young wife.

"Three . . . two. . . one. . . Merry Christmas!" the soldier flipped a large switch, and the tree that stood so regally in the heart of the town transformed before them.

A giant star decorated the top, while red and green lights flickered and flashed. Animated elves skittered around the green branches, and brightly-colored packages danced in a circle below.

Amidst gasps and cries of delight, the crowd cheered again before joining in with the choir to sing "Silent Night."

"Look," said Emma breathlessly. "Isn't it beautiful?"

Noah pressed a kiss to her hair. "It is." He watched his town in all its merriment. "What's your favorite part?"

Like she could pick just one thing. The way harmonies always rose above the melody, even in large crowds. The families bundled together, sipping hot chocolate and grinning from ear to ear. The way the world slowed during moments like these, and for just a few moments, they all shared the same desire to be still, to be quiet, and to leave the ugliness behind. There was the tree that pointed to heaven like a holy evergreen and the stars twinkling down in the clear night sky. As far as the eye could see, candles glowed in the hands of friends, neighbors, and those who had stopped by in search of that elusive Christmas spirit.

"*You* are my favorite part of tonight, Noah," Emma finally decided. "Seeing you so happy here. The expression on your face as you look at the culmination of all your vision and hard work." She blinked back tears. Sugar Creek had made her a veritable bawl baby. "I can't believe I'm standing here with you seeing all of this. I wouldn't have missed this for the world. It's so easy to just go through the motions of the holiday, to not even notice what's around you. But not here in Sugar Creek. You've made us all stop and. . . . just stop." She knew she was barely making sense. "I can feel it—Christmas. The people, the magic, this town. And that's a gift you've given to us all."

Noah might've been there as the Sugar Creek mayor, but he was *her* mayor tonight. She stood on tiptoe and gave him a soft, lingering kiss. She wanted Noah to know how much this night had affected her, how many hearts he had stirred.

Emma knew her own heart would never be the same.

"I love you, Noah Kincaid," she whispered.

Noah lifted his head, and his serious eyes pinned her in place. "Emma—"

"You don't have to say anything." Good heavens, Emma had not meant to say that. It was the lights, the singing, the nostalgia. "I. . . . .I. . . ." She frantically scanned her brain for something eloquent, something more controlled.

Noah stepped closer, shielding Emma's body from the biting wind. "Emma Sutton, I've loved you since our third date, sharing a bowl of greasy nachos in the student union. I knew I still had it bad the day you showed up back in town." He held her gloved hand in his. "I've just been waiting for you to catch up."

When Noah kissed her, Emma felt like her heart was at rest for the first time in her life. All the anger she'd lived with for so long, the bitterness, the guilt she'd dragged behind her like a two-ton anvil had vanished. None of that seemed to matter right now.

"I have to go talk to some folks." Noah pressed a soft kiss to Emma's temple. "We have some pretty big media outlets here that I need to touch base with."

She wanted to stay right where they were and not let reality intrude, but work called. "And I need to check on the ice rink."

The wind ruffled Noah's dark hair. "You and me—we're talking when we get home."

Emma nodded. That seemed to always be where she messed things up. "Right."

After one more swoon-worthy kiss, Noah was gone.

Emma followed the chiming Christmas music and walked down the street that ran in front of the city courthouse. This year Sugar Creek had transformed its splash park into an ice skating rink. It would be open all winter, and judging by ticket sales and the crowds, it was a huge hit.

"How's it going, Bob?" Emma asked the man in an elf hat taking money.

"Hey, Miss Sutton. Man, we're busy. Good idea having Santa skate with the kids tonight." Bob chuckled. "Santa's only fallen ten times. He's gonna need to move some of that padding from his belly to his back side."

"Everything looks great." Emma spied her grandmother and Frannie wobbling on skates, holding one another's arms, and giggling like school girls. Sylvie had one of those laughs that made you smile, even when you had no idea what the punch line was. Emma bought three hot coffees from the teenager in the concession booth, then waved at her grandmother and friend.

"Is that for me?" Sylvie swished past and reached for the railing. She and Frannie unlaced their skates and swapped them for shoes.

Emma handed them their steaming coffees. "You didn't need to quit yet. I was enjoying the show."

Frannie took her first sip. "Just like watching the Ice Capades, eh?"

Emma hid her smiling lips behind her cup. "Just like it."

The three of them leaned on a low wall surrounding the rink and watched the skaters.

"You've done a wonderful job here, Shug," Sylvie said. "This place has been turned into a winter wonderland."

"Noah's done most of the work. I just followed through on the plans already in motion." Emma watched a mother try to coax her young daughter to the ice. "He thinks we've had over ten thousand visitors in the last few weeks."

"I'd call that a success." Sylvie patted Emma's back.

"You gonna marry that mayor of ours?" Frannie asked.

The question spun Emma like a triple lutz. "It's much too soon to be talking about that."

"Honey," Frannie said. "You can't let the good ones get away. You've been sweet on each other since college. It's not like you just started dating."

But they really had. They were two different people now. Or at least Emma was.

"Leave the her alone, Fran," Sylvie said. "They'll figure it out. I'm just working on persuading my girl here to stay in Sugar Creek forever." She patted Emma's cold cheeks. "I've never seen you so happy. Even happier than that time I took you to that boy band concert in Little Rock."

"The one where you pushed me out of the way so you could throw your bra onstage?"

Sylvie blew into her cup. "I'm sure it was a move for your bodily protection."

"You know I have to go back soon," Emma said. "I've sent in most of the video footage and photos I need. I'm about to submit the rest of my copy, then it's just a matter of my boss reviewing it and seeing if I've redeemed my *bah humbug* ways and brought him the Christmas story he wanted." Sugar Creek had turned out to be the perfect haven to get away, to revive her weary spirit, and to deliver *Sunrise News* just what they wanted.

"Well, at least you're here for Christmas," Sylvie said. "That's the best gift a grandma could ask for."

"Except that new Luger pistol," Frannie said. "That thing'll put a turkey on the dinner table."

Those two would never change. "I should go find Noah. I wanted to meet the editor from that magazine he said was here." Emma kissed her grandmother's cheek. "Love you, Sylvie."

Sylvie's smile couldn't hide her motherly concern. "You too, Shug. You too."

Emma enjoyed the stroll back to the square, taking slow steps, giving herself the chance to say hello to people and watch all the activity. In New York, people moved so fast. There were miles to walk, subways to catch, and places to be. But not in Sugar Creek. Not tonight.

It was the first night for movies on the square, and a giant screen had been hung from an old two-story building so families could set up their lawn chairs, cover up with blankets, and watch *Miracle on 34th Street.* She followed the sidewalk back to the middle of the square where the majestic tree blinked brightly enough to make Oklahoma jealous. The local women's choir had taken over the music, and their blends of alto and soprano lilted through the breeze.

Emma saw her father before he noticed her.

He stood with his arm around a woman, their heads bent in intimate conversation.

The child in her wanted to turn on her heel and walk away.

The adult in her knew she needed to go speak.

That adult would probably need a drink later.

Emma approached the couple, not quite able to work up the fake television smile that rarely failed her. "Hi, Dad."

"Emma." His voice was full of jolly tidings. "I was hoping to run into you here. This is my wife, Cheryl."

"It's so nice to meet you," the woman said. She wore a bob much like Emma's mom had, but instead of blonde tresses, Cheryl's was Clairol brown. "Your dad and I watch you on TV all the time."

Emma glanced at her dad. "That's very nice."

"When you interviewed last year's Oscar winners, I just about peed my pants."

Emma smiled at her father's wife. "That would make two of us." She didn't want to like Cheryl, but the woman seemed genuinely kind.

"We're staying out at the hunting lodge on the creek," Emma's father said. "You should come out and have dinner with us tomorrow night."

"Oh, yes!" Cheryl's hands fluttered with every word. "I could cook for us."

"Cheryl's a great cook."

Emma's mother had been as well. "I would like that, but I have to work."

Cheryl gave a dramatic sigh. "Like father, like daughter. This man works all the time. I made him promise to cut back this Christmas. Do you know he's only performing twice a week this month? And he has the entire week of Christmas off."

"That's great." For a woman who had made her living with words, Emma couldn't think of anything beyond the generic.

"I really would love to see you," her father said. "We could catch up. It's been a few years."

"And, of course, I'm so looking forward to getting to know you." Cheryl beamed at Emma like she was one of Hollywood's elite. "Your father talks about you all the time."

He does?

"Don't forget, we're here all month, so we simply must get together," Cheryl said. "Oh, someone seems to be looking for you." She held up her mittened hand and waved. "Hi, there, Mayor Kincaid."

It was like Noah had planted one of Sylvie's eavesdropping devices on Emma. He seemed to know just when she needed him near.

"Noah Kincaid." He extended his arm and shook the couple's hands, then reeled Emma to his side. "It's a pleasure to meet you."

"We were just telling Emma we're staying at the hunting cabins at the edge of town," Edward said. "We'd love to have you two for dinner tomorrow night."

Emma jabbed her elbow into Noah's side. "I mentioned we'd be working pretty late."

"Right." Noah was a terrible liar. "It's a very busy time with all the city preparations."

"It was good to see you, Em," her father said. "I hope you can make time to stop by."

"I'm a hugger," Cheryl said before she put the bear grip on both Emma and Noah. "So, so excited to meet you both!" The woman gave Emma a woman-to-woman wink. "Hang onto that one!"

They both watched them leave. "She's nice," Noah said.

She was also overbearing, space-invading, holiday sweater-wearing, and not her mother. "Yeah."

Noah turned and held out his arms. "I'm a hugger." And before Emma could protest, he had her wrapped in tightly, his chin resting on her head. "Babe, you're as rigid as that giant tree."

Emma closed her eyes, giving over to the battering ram of emotions that always accompanied a visit with her father.

Only this time, it was different. Because now he had a wife. Technically Emma had a stepmother. He couldn't get it together to be a dad, but being a husband again was apparently no problem.

"You okay?" Noah rubbed his hands over her back.

"I'm fine."

"*Fine* as in you want to borrow Sylvie's throwing stars and tear something up, or *fine* as in you think you're going to be okay?"

She smiled against his coat. "It's just hard. On one hand, he's a stranger. But on the other, that was my dad. The dad who came as a set with my mom."

"Where are you at on the whole forgiveness thing?"

Leave it to the attorney to get right to the point. "I'm not sure," Emma said, then asked the question that had begun to haunt her on sleepless nights. "How did you forgive me for what I did?"

Noah's hands stilled, and he took a moment to reply. "I just decided what happened in the past wasn't nearly as important as what I wanted to happen now." He looked at her with so much tenderness and understanding, Emma thought she might break into a million pieces. "He's not going away, Em. You've got to decide where he fits into your life." His eyes darkened as he took a step back. "Probably need to decide where I fit as well."

15

The next few weeks flew by on snowbird wings of bliss. Emma felt like everywhere she went, cartoon hearts surely floated over her head. It was impossible to hide how obscenely happy she was. She and Noah spent every evening together, sometimes going out, maybe to her favorite restaurant in nearby Fayetteville, or just sitting side by side on his couch, both of them working contentedly on their laptops. This was the clean version of "what I do with my evenings," Emma always gave Sylvie. The truth might've been a little steamier, and a whole lot more fun.

Delores just grunted her disapproval at the boss dating his marketing director, but Delores grunted everything from her coffee order to her directions for the jammed copier, so Emma didn't get too concerned.

Sylvie was already picking out matching gun holsters for the wedding she was convinced would eventually happen, but somehow Emma didn't find the thought as amusing as her grandmother did. Emma loved Noah, but every time he broached the subject of their future, she steered the conversation in another direction. How could she tell him the thought of marriage scared her, even if it was with the best man God ever created? More importantly, how did she tell Noah she was in twice-daily talks with her producer at *Sunrise News*, and her invitation to return would come sooner rather than later? Emma wanted Noah to move to New York with her, but she feared she already knew his answer. His life was in Sugar Creek. Could she ask him to give it all up—his job and home he loved—to live in the big city?

Emma stepped into Noah's office for their daily noon date and immediately knew something was wrong.

His tie lay curled like a snake on his desk, his sleeves were rolled to his forearms like a weatherman bracing for a night of storms, and he had clearly shoved his fingers through his disheveled hair more than once.

"And you've checked every flight out of Utah?" Noah said into his phone. "Why would they fly out of Salt Lake in the first place? I thought they were coming from Los Angeles." Noah glanced up at Emma and did not flash her his usual smile. His face looked downright grizzly. "The gala starts at seven, so no, I don't think a bus is going to work unless the band wants to perform at breakfast. Yes, yes, I'm sorry too." Without saying goodbye, Noah clicked off his phone and dropped it to his desk.

"What's wrong?" Emma stepped behind Noah, set her hands to his shoulders, and began to knead at the knotted muscles.

"The band we hired for the gala can't make it. They're snowed in with no way out."

"Oh, no."

Noah had arranged for a popular country group to perform and tickets to the gala had sold out within days.

"There's no way they can be here?" she asked.

"None."

"Maybe I can find someone. I've got a few connections." Emma knew many celebrities, and some of them could possibly be sweet-talked into doing a little pro-bono performance in exchange for future exposure on *Sunrise News*.

"If we don't find someone, I'm letting your grandma sing."

Emma dug her thumbs into Noah's shoulders and smiled. "Her favorite song is 'Machine Gun' by Jimi Hendrix." She placed a soft kiss on Noah's cheek. "Ought to be a real hit."

Emma went back to her office, typed a list of every possible musician or band she knew, then began the difficult task of contacting their reps. People who had people were not easy to track down. Especially four days before Christmas.

When her cell phone rang an hour later, it wasn't her favorite pop artist on the other end but Mr. Peterson, her boss at the show.

"Emma, is this a bad time?"

"Of course not." She put on her most polite voice, filtering out the dread that threatened to accent each word. "What can I do for you?"

"I've reviewed everything you've sent me. I thought we should discuss it."

Her stomach turned as if she'd swallowed spoiled egg nog. "I'd like to hear what you think."

"Well, my dear," Mr. Peterson said, "I think it's fabulous."

Emma's hand froze on her keyboard. "You do?"

"It's everything we could want. Small towns are really hot right now, and that's exactly what you've brought us. The interviews, the photos, the videos—it's all just top notch. The before and after of Sugar Creek is really something, isn't it? I mean this city went from a tiny town with no claim to fame except for a mention in Civil War history books to being on its way to establishing itself as a must-see Christmas road trip."

It was all true, but coming from someone else's lips, someone who had not lived and breathed Sugar Creek, it sounded so cheap, so commercial. "It's a very special town."

"In your last email you mentioned tonight was the gala."

"Yes, our last event." And Emma's last role as the marketing director.

"I dispatched two camera guys to Arkansas this morning. I want to make sure this formal celebration gets quality shots. Rob and Jesse should be there tonight about six-thirty. Can you get them in?"

"Sure," she heard herself say.

"You've done spectacular work, Emma. I couldn't be prouder. Our viewers are going to love this."

"Thank you, sir." Emma's skin tingled with a dark foreboding. Everything Mr. Peterson said was so kind and complimentary. Yet she wasn't ready for her New York life to intrude. She had been living in a snow globe world, going on like everything was perfect between her and Noah, visiting her grandmother whenever she wanted, and doing work that had unexpectedly refilled her empty well.

"Production is already working on your piece. We should have it ready by the time you get back."

There it was. The dreaded date. Emma's return had been something she had fiercely wanted in November. But now? Now she just wished she could press pause on this conversation and this part of her life, and go on for a bit longer with this life in Sugar Creek.

"I have my job back?"

"Of course you do. Sandra has the week of Christmas off, so we'll need you in her seat with Charles."

"Maybe that's a little rushed and—"

"You'll work the day of Christmas Eve as well. That's when we'll air your segment. We're promoting it as our Christmas card to our viewers."

"How . . . clever." Emma's throat tightened, and she just wanted to curl up under the desk and pretend this phone call had never happened. "I had hoped to be with my family for Christmas. I thought my hiatus extended until the first of the year."

"Not anymore!" Mr. Peterson said as if handing Emma a winning lottery ticket. "In fact, I'd like you to go ahead and work the Christmas Day Parade. It will be ideal exposure for you. We need the readers to remember you as their morning sweetheart, and not their holiday Grinch."

"I promised my grandmother I would be with her at Christmas. And my—" What exactly did she call Noah? "My boyfriend is expecting—"

"Emma, if you come through for me on this, and your Christmas story wins over viewers like I think it will, I've got big plans for you. The president is granting us the first interview once he leaves office. I think you could be just the person for the job."

"Me?" She couldn't believe it. Mr. Peterson would assign her to that? No more interviews with over-hyped reality stars and pop divas? "I would love to interview the president. You know I can do it. I am the woman you want for that job."

"It's good to have you back. Tie the ribbon on this Christmas project of ours, and hurry back home."

Emma held the phone in her hands long after the call was over.

Hurry back home.

There was no escaping it—Emma would be returning to New York.

The question was, would Noah go with her?

EMMA CHECKED her directions and turned onto a bumpy dirt road. The creek ran through town and widened near a large expanse of property now owned by Emma's cousin Jack. Jack was another one of Sylvie's grandchildren, though he tended to keep to himself. He had opened a guy's paradise on the outskirts of Sugar Creek where people could stay in a quaint cabin and do all sorts of outdoorsy things on the few hundred acres of property. Hike, fish, mountain bike. Jack would even take folks out to hunt. To Emma, it sounded like a camo-wearing nightmare.

Cabin Number Twelve.

Emma drove past the main house until she saw the one Cheryl had said she and her father were occupying. The place looked rustic, but charming in its rural sort of way.

Her boots crunched on the gravel as she got out of the car. Emma had taken no more than five steps when the door swung open and Cheryl nearly leapt outside.

"Well, get in here darlin'!" Hair in a stubby ponytail, Cheryl ran to Emma and tackled her for a hug. "Don't you smell pretty. You must tell me what perfume you wear sometime. I'm partial to Avon myself."

Emma's dad appeared in the doorway. "Hey, Em."

She took a big gulp of clean, country air. "Hi, Dad."

"Come on in. Cheryl just brewed a fresh pot of coffee."

She stepped inside and noticed her dad and new stepmother had made the place homier than Emma's Manhattan apartment. Though they were staying for only a month, they had put up pictures of the two of them, even a few of Emma. A fire roared in the wood stove, and smells of cinnamon and vanilla wafted from the tiny kitchen.

"I just made a batch of my Snickerdoodles," Cheryl said. "You must have five or ten."

Emma smiled, but turned the offer down. "I'll be returning to work in a few days. I'm afraid I have to return to my carb-free life."

"Well, that sounds just awful." Cheryl bit into a cookie and grinned. "Life's too short to choose a skirt size over cookies."

Easy for her to say. "Dad, can we talk?"

"Sure, hon. Cheryl?"

"I'll just bee-bop out of your way. I've got a Nicholas Sparks book back in the bedroom, and I'm not sure, but I think someone might die in this one."

Edward gestured to a burgundy couch as Cheryl shut herself in a back room. "Want some coffee?"

"No, thank you." Emma sat on the edge of the cushion.

"It must be important. Did you need to talk wedding plans perhaps? You know I'm good for the bill."

Maybe she did need a few cookies. "No, no wedding. I've come here to ask you a favor. I talked to Cheryl, and she said you're not performing tonight."

"Nope. It's one of my wife-mandated nights off."

"I need a favor from you."

"Anything," her father said. "Tell me what you need."

Emma couldn't believe these words were about to come out of her mouth. "I want you to put on a concert at the Sugar Creek Christmas gala."

Her father leaned forward in his chair and offered her his better ear. "Say that again?"

She really didn't want to, but for Noah and Sugar Creek

—anything. "The band scheduled for the gala tonight got snowed in. I've gone through my extensive list of musician contacts, but no one can come to Arkansas this late. I know it's last minute, but . . . would you sing for us tonight?"

"But our agreement. I want to always honor that." Her father muted the television. "I assume you want me to skip a certain song."

"No." What she *wanted* wasn't important. "We both know your song about Mom is the draw. They'll love it." Though she still didn't know why. "These people have paid a lot of money for a fancy dinner and a big name concert. No matter what I think about your career path, you're a very big name. Who better to entertain at a Christmas gala than you?"

"Are you sure?"

"Yes."

"You're pretty desperate here, aren't you?"

Emma smiled with lips that resembled her dad's. "I am."

"I'm still honored you asked me. It's a start, eh?"

"Yes," Emma said. "A start is what it is."

16

It was either a night for magic . . . or an evening for disaster.

Emma adjusted the gold chain at her throat and tried to tune into the conversation at her table.

"You seem a million miles away tonight." Noah rested his arm on the back of her chair and leaned in to whisper in her ear. "Is there something wrong with the food?"

The Sugar Creek Fine Arts Center had been turned into one great big, sparkly dining room. The theater seating had all been removed, and in its place were round dinner tables covered in red and gold tablecloths. For the millionth time, Emma scanned the facility, looking for the *Sunrise News* camera guys. So far they had not shown. Snowy weather had delayed everyone else, why not these guys too?

"No, the catering is excellent. I guess I'm just a little tense over the entertainment."

"Have I told you how profoundly grateful I am that you asked your dad to sing?"

Emma attempted a smile. "At least a dozen times. I think you even offered me your dessert in gratitude."

"I do not recall that part at all." Noah brushed his lips

lightly over hers. "You look stunning tonight, Emma. I'm the luckiest guy in the room."

"Thank you." He had mentioned that a few times as well, but it still did her heart good to hear it. Tonight Emma wore a strapless ruby red gown and her hair swept into an updo that allowed a few wavy tendrils to escape. She had topped the look with her favorite earrings, the delicate diamond studs that had belonged to her mother.

Noah looked like he was ready to walk the Red Carpet in his dashing black tux with a holly berry-red bowtie. He looked just as dashing in formal wear as he did standing on top of her roof hanging lights. No matter the setting, he captured Emma's attention.

"Ladies and gentlemen, once again, we thank you for coming." The emcee, a disc jockey from a local radio station, spoke into the microphone, bringing the room chatter to a low rumble. "As you know the snow has wreaked havoc all over the country, and our scheduled band could not be here. But tonight we have a treat for you. Our own Miss Emma Sutton, who has worked so tirelessly with our mayor to make Sugar Creek a Christmas dream, arranged for a very special guest to perform tonight. And that guest is . . .her *father*!" His arm extended toward the curtain. "Please welcome Edward Casey!"

The surprised crowd applauded, and Emma held her smile in place as people swiveled in their seats to see her reaction.

"Good evening." Emma's father grinned and held his guitar. "I'm honored to be here with you tonight. But more importantly, I'm honored to be the father of that pretty young woman right there."

Noah's arm around Emma tightened as Edward pointed right to her to the sound of more cheers.

"I thought I'd open with a few traditional favorites."

Emma released a breath as the lights dimmed, and her father began to play a tune that was not one of his own.

Noah's brow furrowed. "Emma, who is that?"

She followed the path of Noah's focused gaze and knew the network cameramen had arrived.

"Are those the guys you hired for PR?"

"No," Emma whispered. "They're from *Sunrise News*. My boss called me today." She gave a humble shrug. "Turns out he loves my story on Sugar Creek. He wanted professional footage of the gala."

Noah's jaw tightened. "When were you going to mention this?"

"You knew I was working on it."

He leaned closer until his lips were next to her ear. "What else did your boss say?"

"Can we talk about this later?"

"I was thinking we should've talked about it *earlier*."

She could barely hear him over the cords from her father's guitar. "We've both had a lot to handle today. You with the gala situation, and me with my dad. I just wanted tonight to be a nice evening, Noah." Her eyes pleaded with him to let it drop. "Can we discuss this after the gala's over?"

Emma didn't know how many songs her father played—seven? Eight? They all sounded the same to her, but when she heard him strum the opening intro of one tune, the few bites of chicken she'd swallowed at dinner threatened to stage a rebellion.

"You know the story," Edward said, as if talking to a few of his closest friends. "Many years ago I lost my beloved first wife on Christmas. That holiday became the anniversary for one of the darkest moments in my life. And in my daughter's, as well. As a father, you can't imagine what it's like to see your child suffer." Emma's dad looked right at her. "To see her heart shatter and know there's not one thing you can do." His fingers began to play the melody. "But I was hurting too. And that Christmas night, I penned these words."

The cameramen swooped in, crouching low to stay out of the way, but close enough to capture this sentimental gold.

"Excuse me." Emma placed her napkin on the table, and with a smile for the dignitaries seated at her table, she stood and walked out of the theater.

The speakers amplified her father's words, and like a taunting bully, those painful lyrics chased her down the hall.

Why didn't God answer my prayer?
Why didn't Santa Claus care?
All I asked was for my momma to be well . . .

"Emma, wait."

Behind her, Noah was hot on her heels.

"Just give me a minute," she called, not bothering to look back. Lord, she needed air. And lots of it.

She burst through the exit doors like the building behind her was disintegrating into flames, her heels clicking on the pavement. A small fountain gurgled at the edge of the property, and Emma finally stopped there. Eyes closed, she rubbed the tension in her temples, and tried to wipe that stupid song from her brain.

"Are you okay?" Noah reached for Emma, but she shrugged away.

"Yes."

The water spit and arced, and Emma noticed the pennies people had tossed in, hoping to have a change in luck. So many wishes, she couldn't see the bottom of the fountain.

"I'm fine, Noah," she said. "I just needed to get some fresh air."

He settled his tuxedo jacket over her shoulders, but made no other move to touch her. "I know it still hurts you."

"It's just a stupid song. That was the worst moment of my life, and he turned it into this hokey, cheesy, horribly-written disaster. I mean, he rhymed *cancer* with Blitzen and Dancer."

"It's not exactly 'O Holy Night.' "

"I told him he could sing it. That's what everyone wants to hear. But it just takes me right back to that day. And then I remember all the years he made me go on tour and sit on the stage like a total puppet." Thank God Sylvie had finally intervened.

"You're clearly not over it." Noah stood behind Emma, so close she could feel his heat at her back.

"Maybe that's what I'm most upset about. I'm thirty-freaking-one, and I thought I was past this." She turned and faced him. "But she was a real person, you know—my mom. Not this fabled character in Edward's song. She had a heart and a soul and a life. She was full of joy and light. We'd sit together at the piano and sing carols." Emma sang alto, while her mother had provided the beautiful soprano that had made her the star of the church choir.

Emma let the tears fall unchecked. "I remember sitting on her lap on Christmas Eve as she'd read the Christmas story. Then we'd all crash on the couch near the fire. I'd be wearing my new pajamas, and Mom would sit with me and let me talk about what I thought was under the tree. She had the most beautiful laugh." Her own laugh was small, broken. "She loved Christmas."

"It's understandable that it's still a hard," Noah said.

Emma pulled his jacket tighter, unable to get warm.

"This has been the most special holiday season I've ever had since she died. All thanks to you." She reached out her hand to caress his cheek, but his eyes seemed to lack their usual warmth.

"Your father doesn't mean to hurt you with his song," Noah said. "He might never get it."

"You're right. He probably never will." Emma sat on the edge of the fountain, the chill of the concrete seeping into her dress. "Let's talk about something else. Anything. You can even talk about your boring sports stuff."

Noah did not smile. He did look right at Emma, with eyes that held his own measure of hurt. "Let's discuss what's going to happen with us."

Emma suddenly craved a good discussion on football helmet safety or who was favored to win the next championship. "We love each other. We're in a relationship."

"Are we?"

Oh, she did not like that tone. It said *danger, land mines ahead.* "Why are we discussing this now?"

"Because I think you have something to tell me."

He was good.

Noah had always known when she was collecting secrets like posies between the pages of a book. "You *know* I wanted to stay here for Christmas."

"Just spit it out, Emma."

Emma knew the words would change everything. "My boss wants me back at work immediately."

"And you told him you were staying here through the holiday, right?"

She slowly shook her head. "I have to go back. They've ended my hiatus, and they're running the Sugar Creek story on the twenty-fourth."

"And you have to be there for that?"

"It's my story. And the first step in winning back my viewers' favor." By the time the segment aired, America would know everything about Sugar Creek's Christmas, as well as Emma's own disastrous history with the holiday.

"So you're going back to New York."

"Yes." She hated the disappointment and wariness staring back at her. "I've always been honest about that, Noah. My job is there."

"A job you don't even want."

"I have a promotion coming soon." She sounded so defensive, even to her own ears. "I have to go back."

"And where does that leave us, Emma?" He was looking at her just like he had the first night she'd returned to town.

Sometimes you marched to the battle lines, even knowing victory was not within your reach. "Come with me. Noah." She stood, her fingers circling his wrist. "Come with me to New York."

He stared at the ground and rubbed the back of his neck. "No." Noah lifted his head and met Emma's gaze. "I can't go with you."

"Why?"

His stormy eyes held no mercy now. "Who will you and I be in New York?"

"A couple in a committed relationship."

He shook his head. "I think only one of us would be committed."

"How can you say that?"

"Because this is history repeating itself." Noah removed her hand from his. "Only this time you're allowing me to tag along."

Emma blinked against the blowing wind and the slap of his words. "This is *not* ten years ago. I'm not that person anymore."

"I had hoped you weren't."

"So if I stay here and support your career, then my love is believable. I'm worthy to stay with you. But if I ask you to come with me, I'm just that silly college girl who ran. I have a career in New York. It's not like I can do that level of work just anywhere. You can be an attorney in New York. You're choosing this town over me."

Noah's voice was so resolute. "I would follow you anywhere if I thought you were all in."

"I *am* all in."

"You're following a job that might be incredibly prestigious, but it kills you every day. You don't even like it. Have the guts to walk away from that and be something else. Be anything. I'm not going back to New York so you can work fifteen-hour days, seven days a week for a job you can't stand, but stick with because it supports your addiction of avoiding people trying to love you."

His words shot like an arrow, piercing the fragile target of her heart. "You just want your job to take precedence."

"What needs to take precedence for this to work is *us*. And you've never been able to commit to that. Even when we were in school, I was an afterthought."

"I loved you." Emma still did. Didn't he see that?

Anger flashed in his eyes. "You left me."

"We were young," she said. "I just felt claustrophobic. I needed some space."

"You moved across the country." His laugh was completely devoid of mirth. "I'd say you found it."

"I did love you." Maybe if she repeated it over and over, Noah would see. He'd believe her and change his mind.

"Love doesn't run, Emma."

"I wanted more than this town. Your dream was always to come back here."

"With *you*. My dream was to come back home with you."

"It was always your plan. What about mine?"

"You should've talked to me."

"I tried. You never listened. You knew I wanted to make my career a priority. I couldn't be a top news anchor and stay in a small town in Arkansas."

"You had a communications degree, yet you couldn't tell me in person you were leaving. I got home from work and found a letter and your engagement ring."

"I'm so sorry." She had panicked, exactly like she was now. "That wasn't the right way to handle it."

"No, it wasn't. The right way would've involved us sitting down and having a conversation, you telling me you were ending our engagement. You looking me in the eyes and explaining to me what I'd done wrong. Giving me a chance to fix it."

"I'm asking you to help me fix it now."

"I don't think you are. You're going back to something I can't fix. You told me your job left you empty, that it made you unhappy."

"But I would be crazy to pass up this opportunity."

"You're not going back because you love the work and because it's what you want to do. I'd follow you all over the world for that. But you're going back because it's familiar."

"Won't you even give this a shot?"

"You know what I think?" Noah paced a few steps in front of Emma. "I think I scare you. The thought of a future together scares you. You get twitchy at the very idea of putting roots down here. Sugar Creek to you is permanence. It's a husband, it's family, it's . . . me."

Tears gathered on Emma's lashes, and she blinked against the pressure. She was losing Noah. He was walking away. "Please don't do this," she whispered.

"I'm not your father. I'm not going to disappear when things get rough. I'm not going to be distant and send checks and call it love. And I sure as heck wouldn't let someone else take my place and not fight for you."

She wanted to believe that so much. "I do love you, Noah Kincaid. Try and understand—"

"You tell me that TV show fills you up, makes you happy, and I'll go, Emma. You tell me that you're on board with the idea that we're on a trajectory that involves marriage, permanence, and I'll go."

Emma heard the faint sound of her father's voice drift from the auditorium. "Just let me take this one step at a time."

"No." Noah stood there, wind blowing his hair, his stance stiff and unyielding. "You decide what you really want and how committed you are. I let the past go, Emma, but you never have. I may not still be the twenty-one-year-old boy who found his fiancée gone and his ring left behind." He shook his head, and Emma knew it was over. "But you are still that girl."

17

Snow fell in delicate, gossamer flakes the next afternoon. Emma held out her hand and caught a few. So tiny, so fragile.

So temporary.

Bags packed in her new rental, Emma set out early for the airport. She had cried when Sylvie hugged her. Her grandmother hadn't begged her to stay for Christmas, only said she understood. But how could she? Emma didn't even know if *she* understood.

The nativity wasn't on her way, but Emma's car seemed to pull her there. Her face lifted into the elements as she walked to the manger, letting the snow fall across her skin like a Christmas baptism. There was Mary, studying her child, a Mona Lisa lift of her lips. Joseph stood behind his wife and clasped her shoulders, as if to say, *well done there.* The Wise Men held their gifts, and Emma idly wondered what the family had thought of their offerings. Maybe Mary had just wanted a good candy bar and a suite at the Holiday Inn.

Or maybe Mary was too transfixed by the sight of the

newborn child to even care what she had endured, what heartache had led her to that point. Perhaps the beauty of her child washed it all away. When Mary looked into the face of her baby, did she see a precious infant she wanted to hold forever, or did she see . . . God? God and a plan so much bigger than anything she could wrap her human mind around?

Emma stood by Mary and ran her fingers down the young mother's arm. Perhaps it was enough to know that if things were uncertain, even frightening, that God was upstairs saying, "*Hey, I got this. Just keep walking.*"

She clutched that hope close. Because the thought of leaving her career, just laying down all that she had worked so hard for, was absolutely terrifying. If she stayed in Sugar Creek, her career was uncertain, her reputation as a journalist—gone. What would she have?

The only known was Noah.

Noah would be there. And the rest of her family. Sylvie, her cousins.

Digging into her purse, Emma pulled out a convenience store receipt, then picked some more until her fingers touched a pen. Like all the dreamers, wishers, and hopers, she would add a prayer to the manger.

Emma closed her eyes and listened to the mix of silence and hush that only snowflakes could make. She breathed in the smell of the crisp air and imagined the glowing lights were like a holiday card just for her. A prayer whispered from her lips—a plea, a praise. A wisp of impossibility.

Opening her eyes, Emma set her pen to the crinkled paper.

It was her Christmas wish.

Something so precious she hardly dared to give it life with her inky swoops and swirls.

Though it was a little foolish, Emma kissed the paper with chapped lips, wished it Godspeed, then placed it in the manger.

Twenty-three years ago, a young Emma had offered up a prayer. It had meant everything to her. She had childishly thought if God hadn't heard her spoken requests, maybe he would finally get the word in writing. Maybe he just wanted a bit of mail.

Emma's small hands had tucked the card beneath the arm of the baby Jesus. The manger had held her prayer and the contents of her whole heart.

And yet her mother had died.

Now, she stood there a thirty-one-year-old woman, tears free-falling intermittently like the snow, and once again she came with a beggar's portion of words she feared were not enough.

"I left a prayer too, you know."

Emma turned at that familiar voice.

Bundled in a heavy coat, her father approached the nativity. "I drove by and thought that was you. Tough night?"

"Yes," was all she gave him. "Thank you for the concert."

Her father cleared his throat and scuffed the ground with the toe of his shoe. "You know, the Christmas your mom died, I left my wish in the nativity as well. I placed it right in the manger, and when I did, I saw that familiar Hello Kitty stationery of yours." His smile was bittersweet. "Your words broke my heart."

Emma looked at her father's face, now etched with lines she hadn't been a part of. "I could've used a dad that Christmas."

"I suppose you could've used one your whole life."

There was no arguing with that.

"The one thing you asked for Christmas, and I couldn't give it to you."

"Nobody could," Emma said.

He stared into the manger, as if needing a moment to absorb her words. "As a spouse and a parent, you feel responsible. You want to fix it. And I couldn't. After your mom was gone, I would catch you looking at me, and I knew you were thinking, 'Why didn't God take him instead?'"

She had thought exactly that. "I was hurt and angry. There's no grief like losing your mother." It was in a category all of its own.

"I never got over that feeling of failure," her father said. "I hadn't just lost a wife, but I had lost my daughter as well."

"It didn't have to be that way." How many ways had Emma tried to catch his attention, to get him to act like he saw her?

"I chose the job over my family," he said. "Work didn't judge me, you know? Didn't look at me with those haunted eyes that begged me to turn back the clock." Edward rested a tentative hand on Emma's shoulder. "I'm so sorry, Emma."

Emma searched the inner reserves for the energy to be mad, but found there wasn't much left. "I'm sorry for the way things turned out too."

"You remind me of your mother so much," Edward said. "You have her wavy hair, her laugh. Her love of chocolate and trivia. But I'm afraid to tell you, when I look at you, I also see myself."

She sighed. "It's the nose, isn't it?"

Her father smiled. "It's your wanderlust. Well, actually in the last few years I've come to realize that's not exactly what it is. I think it's more about our staying on the move so we don't have to put down roots and commit to anyone."

"This is kind of a heavy conversation for a little goodbye chat."

But her dad pressed on. "It's easy to walk away from people, even the ones you love. But hear me when I say what you find on the other side will never fill the emptiness, the loneliness. I'd be lying if I said I didn't like my work. I've traveled the world, met amazing people, made more money than I could spend. But when I'd get back to the hotel every night, it was just me." He reached into his pocket and retrieved his wallet. With pinched fingers, he pulled out a faded photo of a smiling family. Just like the one dangling from Emma's tree.

"I've kept this by my bedside every night since I hit the road. I wanted to be enough for that little girl in the picture. But without your mom, I never was. She was always enough parent for both of us. All I knew how to do was work."

That perma-frosted corner of Emma's heart dripped just a little at the sight of the photo. "You could've tried."

"But I didn't." His voice faltered. "And I didn't get any do-over. Don't you think I'd like to wake up tomorrow, be thirty years old again, and take a different path?"

"What would you do differently?" Emma needed the words. Needed to know she mattered.

"I would've stayed, Emma. I would read some of those parenting books or taken a class or something. Made it work."

She voiced her fear to the one person who might get it. "I don't know if I'm the settle-down kind of person," she admitted. "Maybe I do get that from you." *Thank you very much, Dad.*

Edward clasped Emma's shoulders. "Do you love this Noah fellow?"

"Yes." Of that she was certain. "But maybe it's not enough. It's just—it's very frightening."

"Then you stay here—scared.You be honest and tell him you don't know how to stick it out, but you're going to." His eyes held hers. "Emma, you're going to mess up, maybe a lot. You're going to get mad and need your space and fall on your face. But at the end of the day, you'll know that tomorrow you're going to try again. That's what I wish I would've done—tried."

She wished he had as well. "I would've loved you, you know."

Edward nodded like he did know. "Your mom was so perfect, such a natural. I guess I thought if I didn't do it right, I shouldn't do it at all. But that's not how it works, is it?"

"I was a kid," Emma said. "All I wanted was you."

"And I'm betting all Noah wants is you." He father picked up a card from the nativity floor and read. When he lifted his eyes to hers again, Emma saw the same weariness, the same regret she carried inside. "Em, you tell me what you like about work, what's pulling you back to New York."

Emma bristled at the topic change and had to take a moment to answer. "I guess it's all I've known. I'm good at it. It's given me accolades and attention."

"All the care I didn't."

She shrugged. "When I go back to that anchor desk, I know what to expect. I can depend on my job."

"That sounds very romantic."

"I didn't know I was supposed to write a Harlequin for you here."

"I chose a career over love. I chose fear over love. And I made two people very miserable in the process. Emma, tell Noah how you feel. You can make millions of dollars; you can be the best news anchor the world has ever seen. But if you don't have love, what's the point?" Edward pointed a thumb to his down-filled chest. "Sweetheart, your Ghost of Christmas Future stands right in front of you. And I'm telling you I know how the news story of Emma Sutton ends. I messed up. I never made it right. But you, my dear? You have the chance to fix this. To create a whole new life for yourself—one with love, laughter, and a family."

Emma sniffed and wiped the falling tears. "But I'm so close to taking over that lead anchor chair. I thought Noah could share that with me."

"Did he make you choose?"

"He said if he thought I truly loved my work, he would go. He said I was running." She wiped her nose with her glove. "He didn't even tell me goodbye."

"If you love that job, you go. And you be the best news anchor this country's ever seen. But sweetheart, if that's not what you want, all that money and all that achievement will make you more bitter than anything I ever did." Edward hugged his daughter to him. "Your mom would be so proud of you."

The tears blurred her eyes.

"But she would also want you happy," her father said. "That's what she'd want from you most of all. Em, it's time to stop filling your trophy case and just live your life."

Emma gave her dad a quick kiss, something she hadn't done in decades. "Take care of yourself, Dad."

"I loved you then, kid," he said. "I'm gonna love you forever."

18

"Hello, Miss Sutton." The doorman in her apartment building lifted his hand in greeting. "We've missed you."

"Thank you, Thomas." Emma smiled at the man, then took in the sight of the lobby. People coming and going, oblivious to everyone around them. No one but Thomas even made eye contact. She already missed the warm greetings of one small town.

"I'll have someone bring your bags up."

"Thank you." She pressed something into his hand. "A little tip for your trouble."

Thomas opened his palm and his eyes went wide. "Merry Christmas, Miss Sutton."

"Merry Christmas to you." It was such a new feeling—to say the words and actually mean them.

Emma pulled her weary body away from the elevator wall when the doors dinged and opened on her floor. She smiled at the couple completely ignoring her on the ride up and walked to her door.

Just one step inside her darkened apartment, and Emma felt the weight of the tears. It was pitiful really. Her apartment was free of all holiday decor, something she never thought she'd miss. No horrible music about toys and snow. No blinking lights her blinds couldn't quite block out while she was trying to sleep. No lopsided tree put up by some giggling women with too much time on their hands.

No Sylvie.

No Noah.

No one.

Emma flopped onto the leather couch and let her body melt into it. She cradled a pillow in her arms and let the tears have their way. This was what she had wanted, she reminded herself. Tomorrow would be the beginning of a new phase of her life. She had her seat on the couch with her morning team. She was on track for lead anchor when Sandra retired. And she lived in the most exciting city in the country.

Closing her eyes, Emma imagined Noah's arms around her—his kiss, his strength, his voice. The ache was as palpable as a punch to the stomach.

Noah had said she was running, but she wasn't. Her life would be good. He just didn't understand. Maybe he would change his mind. Maybe he would come to New York one day. He could practice law, and she would sit in her spot on the *Sunrise News* couch, her permanent smile firmly in place.

Her very fake television smile.

No, tomorrow would be better. Surely Emma had only been experiencing burnout in the last year. Knowing her boss and co-workers were behind her would renew her energy. Tomorrow Emma would have her job back. She would have the esteem of her peers, a new enthusiasm, and even a small raise.

She'd have everything.

Everything except Noah Kincaid.

ON DECEMBER TWENTY-FOURTH, Emma sat in the *Sunrise News* studio in her designer dress, professionally-styled hair, flawless makeup, and some pointy-toed shoes that she could barely stand in. From her seat on the famous red couch, she watched the monitor, a smile teasing her lips at the sight of Sugar Creek on the screen. Charles Chambers, lead anchor and journalistic icon sat to her left, his brown eyes watching every detail, even though she knew he'd not only already seen it, but had given final approval.

The dedicated production staff had turned Emma's video, photos, and reflections into a love letter to a corner of Arkansas and the world. Emma caught a glimpse of Sylvie and Frannie skating at the ice rink and knew they were packing heat under their bulky winter coats. She spied her cousins and their families, talking and laughing over hot chocolate downtown. There was Trent, the wounded soldier who had lit the community Christmas tree. The children's choir. Snow falling on the nativity. The gala. The town square. Even the few seconds of a scowling Delores somehow had Emma sniffling back homesick tears.

Her father's words tiptoed into her thoughts as her segment played.

"Your Ghost of Christmas Future stands right in front of you. And I'm telling you I know how the news story of Emma Sutton ends . . ."

She missed Sylvie. She missed Sugar Creek.

But she was dying without Noah.

The piece ended, and Charles nodded in appreciation.

"Truly an inspiring town," he said. "What a picturesque place to visit."

Picturesque? It was so much more than that. "This was a real homecoming for me. I didn't expect to fall back in love with Sugar Creek, but I did." She also hadn't expected to fall back in love with Noah, the man who had occupied her every thought since she'd left. "You know, Charles, I went to Sugar Creek to find a holiday human interest story, but it turns out . . . *I'm* the Christmas story."

Charles was so professional, so trained, his reaction to Emma's going off script couldn't possibly be perceptible to those watching at home. He laughed jovially and crossed his other leg. "It's no secret how you felt about this time of year. I'm sure the town of Sugar Creek could warm even the strongest of cynics."

She shot the producer an apologetic look, but barreled through. "I have an unusual history with Christmas. As a child, I lost my mother to cancer on Christmas. I'm the daughter of a famous musician with a very famous—or infamous—holiday song. December twenty-fifth has always been the anniversary of some pretty upsetting moments in my life. But going back home, I discovered it was time to make new memories. I worked elbow-to-elbow with community members in the soup kitchen serving a turkey dinner. I spent time with my family, something I hadn't done in years. I celebrated the holiday with hundreds of people I can call friends. I even reconnected with my father."

"I loved you then, kid."

Her father had thought he'd loved her, but love didn't abandon. If that was what he called love, she wanted no part of it. And wasn't that what she was doing to Noah? Giving him her love in words, just like her dad, but leaving Noah behind to chase a career she no longer craved.

Had the set lights ever been this hot? "I guess sometimes the holidays are as miserable as you want to make them," Emma said. "And I've spent a lifetime assuming that was the only option available. This season, I had a chance to give back, to see how much joy Christmas could bring to a town that was counting on one beautiful holiday."

"That's wonderful, Emma. It's like our own *A Christmas Carol* here at *Sunrise News*."

"My time in Sugar Creek woke me up to what I'd been lacking. Like Ebenezer Scrooge, I have some changes to make as well. I cannot go back to being the person I was."

Her heart beat loudly, galloping wildly in her ears. Emma felt her cheeks redden and heat work its way up her neck. It was like a bubbling volcano, this impulse that was pushing to the surface, a force she could not stop.

She had been wrong to leave Sugar Creek.

Noah asked her what she wanted. She wanted him. A life with him.

He told her he would've followed her anywhere, but he was right. She might've had a job most women would envy, but she didn't want it. For all the opportunity and money, it could never make her happy.

Emma had walked away from Noah long time ago, and God had given her the miracle of a second chance. And if it wasn't already too late, she was going to take it.

Today.

Emma looked right into camera two and committed television career suicide.

"This job has been wonderful." Her voice grew stronger. "I've traveled the world. I've met amazing people. I have incredible coworkers, and most importantly, our viewers have become like extended family. You've welcomed me into your homes, and we've walked through some fascinating events together. But this morning"—Her hands shook like the trees that lined the creek running through her town—"I must say goodbye. I didn't just leave my hometown in Arkansas. I left my family. And . . . I left the love of my life."

Emma ignored the waving arms of her producer and continued talking. She was finally certain of something, and she wanted the world to know. "I was happier back home than I've ever been, even with all hustle and stress of the season. I've had one of the best jobs in the world, and I'm so incredibly blessed to have gotten to this point in my career. And as crazy as it sounds to walk away, my heart is somewhere else. Friendship, community, love—I don't want that just in December. I want it all year long. So, it is with an anxious but *certain* heart . . . that I tell you goodbye." Emma's lips lifted in a watery smile. "And from the bottom of my soul, have a very merry Christmas."

19

"What do you mean the flight already left?" Emma leaned over the Dallas American Airlines gate desk, an exhausted, limp mess. She had paid an exorbitant amount of money to get a last-minute flight out of LaGuardia yesterday, leaving straight from work. There were few direct flights to Northwest Arkansas, so she had been forced to connect at Chicago of all places.

A snowstorm had grounded everyone in Chicago, so she'd spent one fitful night in an uncomfortable chair, her phone dead, and trying to keep a snoring man off her shoulder. Her dress wrinkled and uncomfortable beyond repair, Emma had gone shopping during her extended layover and bought some Chicago Bulls pajama bottoms, a *Wicked* hoodie, and a t-shirt that said *Chicago is for Lovers*.

Finally, this afternoon, wrung-out, cranky, and too nervous to even read the *People* magazine sticking from her purse, Emma had been hit with yet another hurdle in her caper to get home.

"I'm sorry," the uniformed woman said as she typed into

her computer. "Your flight from Chicago was over two hours late, and you missed your connection. It's gone."

"We had to fuel up. Then they had to switch planes." For all the time it had taken, the pilot had probably worked in some last minute Christmas shopping as well. "You have no idea what it's taken to get here. Please, you have to find me another flight to Bentonville. I've got to get there by Christmas."

The woman lifted an unsympathetic brow. "Last time I checked the sad voicemails from my kids, it *is* Christmas."

"I'm sorry you have to work. Truly." Emma had worked every holiday. She understood. "But it's so important I'm home by midnight." The long run of terrible holidays ended this year. She was determined to be in Sugar Creek for Christmas, telling Noah exactly how she felt.

"There are no more flights," the gate agent said. "We can get you a voucher for food and a hotel for—"

"I don't want another voucher." Her voice was so whiny, it was barely recognizable. "I have to get to Arkansas." Emma checked the time on her phone. It was already four o'clock. In eight hours Christmas would be over.

"There might be a few rental cars available, but I doubt it."

"Where do I find one?"

The woman pointed south. "Take the escalator down. Good luck."

Emma didn't care that her bags were somewhere in the guts of the airport. There was no time to get them. She grabbed her carryon and purse, pulled off the horrible, pointy-toed heels she'd been coaxed into yesterday morning, and ran through the Dallas airport, dodging in and out of fellow travelers, shoes in hand. Her hair had long been thrown into a top knot, she had washed her TV makeup off back at La Guardia, and she was pretty sure she was sweating right through her new outfit.

Her boss had immediately gone to commercial after her surprise announcement. So while America watched an advertisement for bladder protection or pillowy insoles, Emma sat in her producer's office while he terminated her employment. She'd reminded him she had already quit, but Mr. Peterson hadn't heard a word she'd said.

Emma knew quitting on live TV had been the ultimate in unprofessionalism. She'd already received a hundred texts and calls from friends in the business, wanting to know if she'd lost her mind. A fellow anchor from CBS had left a message of support, love, and the number of a doctor who could "*prescribe you something for that*."

She had handled today in an abysmal fashion.

And yet she'd never felt more free.

Yes, she would take that marketing job.

Yes, she would love Noah for the rest of her days.

And yes, she would like to build a life in Sugar Creek, Arkansas.

Ten minutes later, after dumping her heels in the trash, Emma bought some fuzzy slippers for her feet and found the car rental desk. She pounded her palm against a tiny bell. "Hello? Hello?"

A man wearing a black vest with a rental car logo finally appeared behind the counter. "We're closed."

"No, you can't be. I have to get to Arkansas."

"Lady, it's Christmas. We closed an hour ago, and if I don't get home in time to eat my mother-in-law's dried-out turkey, my wife won't talk to me for a week."

Emma dug in her bag for a few crisp hundred dollar bills, then slid them his way.

The man's beady eyes checked right and left, then

slipped the cash into his pocket. "A week without the wife's yapping actually won't be too bad."

"Thank you." Emma melted against the counter, grateful for the change in fortune. "I'll take whatever you have."

"Good. Because all we have is a twenty-person conversion van. Super handy if you happen to be traveling with a rock band, like the last people to use the vehicle. In fact, my boy Joe hasn't even had time to clean the—"

"I don't care. I'll take it as is."

"I can't give it to you dirty. It's against policy."

Emma handed the guy another twenty. "Let's get that paperwork going, okay?"

He grinned, revealing two missing teeth. "We'll have you on the road before you can say Acid Puppies Death Cry."

Emma blinked. "Why would I say that?"

He shrugged. "It's the name of the band who had the van. Those were some crazy guys."

Thirty minutes later Emma pulled onto the interstate, her hands on the steering wheel of a van that reeked of cigarette smoke, gas station burritos, and a potent mix of illegal substances. A pair of red thong panties dangled from the rearview mirror, Solo cups littered two of the four backseats, and someone had written *Rock-N-Roll Anarchy* in squeeze cheese on the dash. She popped the top on a can of something that promised to keep her energized for six hours, and turned the radio from a screamo station to something a little more mellow.

Nearly every station played Christmas tunes.

Well, who needed music?

Emma turned the thing off. She might've been a new convert to Christmas, but that didn't mean she was ready to love and cherish every single thing about the holiday. She still didn't like carols. Or egg nog. Or the onesie pajamas her grandmother insisted on sending her every year.

Two hours in, Emma took a wrong turn.

Three hours later, her energy drink reneged on its neon promise.

By hour four, she was at least in Arkansas, but the fog had slowed her and the rest of the sparse traffic to speeds reserved for dirt roads and Sunday drives.

By hour five, she called Noah, but it went straight to voice mail. Emma pulled over on the side of the road and cried.

Hour six had her singing along to an Acid Puppies Death Cry CD she'd found beneath the seat and wishing for a cigarette and gas station burrito.

But by 11:50 p.m., running on fumes and sheer willpower, Emma pulled the giant van into Noah's driveway.

She didn't care that she smelled like someone else's sweat or that her top-knot was now a limp appendage hanging from the side of her weary head. And who cared if she was a walking fashion disaster? Emma was at Noah's.

She was home.

But unfortunately Noah Kincaid was not.

She hammered her fist to the door and laid on the doorbell, but no one came. She tried his phone again and again, but only his recorded voice answered.

Noah was gone.

An exhausted whimper escaped her lips as she climbed back into the van of stench and debauchery. She would drive to Sylvie's and get some sleep. There was nothing left to do.

Emma prayed the red light on the gas gauge was just a friendly little warning, as there was no gas station open in Sugar Creek on Christmas. The town still glowed in all its tiny light glory, and even with her eyes swollen in fatigue, Emma smiled at the sight. She drove past the Kiwanis Club display, with its intricate scene of kids opening gifts. The high school's science and technology club's laser show still impressed. And downtown looked like a Rockwell painting outlined in white. The Star of Bethlehem beamed down on the nativity, and Emma slowed the van to get the last look of the season at dear Mary staring so contentedly at her child.

Instead she saw a familiar figure reaching into the manger.

Emma rubbed her burning eyes and peered closer. Someone was out there.

And that someone was Noah.

She whipped the van into a parking spot and flung open her door, punk music shrieking out like a terrible soundtrack to the scene unfolding. And this scene included Noah, Jesus, and if Emma heard right, a song titled, "Chain Me With Your Electric Nose Hairs."

"Noah!" Emma's slippered feet hit the cold pavement. "Noah!"

He turned, his frown visible from thirty feet away. "Emma?"

She couldn't seem to quit nodding her head. *It's me! It's really me. The girl who loves you. The girl who needs you.*

The sleep-deprived girl who smells like the inside of a tenth grader's gym bag.

Emma stopped when she was a mere arm's length away. Just one reach and she could touch him.

But she didn't. Because Noah stood there, hands in his coat pockets, and just stared.

"Hi." She really needed a Tic-Tac. "Did I make it?"

He looked down at her Dallas Cowboy house shoes. "What are you doing here, Emma?"

"What time is it?"

"I don't—" He huffed in frustration, his breath a plume of chilly air. "It's eleven fifty-seven."

Relief sang through Emma's whole body. "I made it. I made it here for Christmas. But why are you at the nativity?"

Noah still regarded Emma like he wasn't sure she was operating on a full tank. "Some lady called about another possible doll theft. The good one got taken again." He glanced down at the manger at the baby with the globe of frizzy red hair. "But nobody seems to want to steal her."

Emma swallowed and licked her lips. It was go-time. "I have to get this all in before midnight, but I need to tell you that I love you. "I don't want to live without you. You love Sugar Creek, and I love Sugar Creek, and I want to build a life here with you. You were right, Noah." Fatigue seemed to delete every eloquent word she had prepared on the long drive.

"I didn't love my job," she said, plodding on. "And I was using it as a filler. I thought it would make me happy at some point, but you know what? Years had gone by, and it never really had. But I was scared. That job was so significant, and I wanted to be more than the daughter in a cheesy Christmas song. I wanted accomplishments—exclusive interviews, killer ratings, a Daytime Emmy—and okay I still kind of want the Emmy. But I just filled my days with work and more work. And where did it get me?"

Noah took a step to her. "You tell me."

Oh, his voice. Emma couldn't wait to wake up to that voice and go to bed at night with that voice. "It got me a very nice apartment that was never a home. Just a place to sleep in because I was never there. I couldn't even get a cat because I was away so much. Even a fish required more care than I could give it. I'm telling you right now, Noah, I want a darn cat. And a fish. But maybe not together."

His brow furrowed in beautiful concern. "Are you on something?"

"No. Well, not technically. But I would not sniff too heavily in that van. Noah, you said you would follow me anywhere if I was all in." Emma reached out and clutched his coat sleeves. "I'm all in. I quit my job. Then I hopped on a plane—a few planes actually. Then I drove like a million miles. Because I love you." *Why wasn't he saying anything?*

"I had this elegant speech all planned out. But then everything turned upside down, and I went from starring in a nice Hallmark romance to some new version of *Planes, Trains, and Automobiles*." Emma's chest rose and fell in marathon-running heaves. "I honestly do not remember what I was going to say." She searched her brain and came up with nothing. "But it was good. Like amazing good." Emma waited for Noah to say something. Anything.

"Was it Emmy-worthy good?" A smile tipped Noah's lips, and Emma felt the breath return to her body.

"Oh, wow. The star still leads."

"What?"

Hope was still alive. "I'm sorry for everything I said. I didn't expect to come back to Sugar Creek, and I sure never dreamed I would lose my heart to you again. But it happened."

Noah slipped his hand over her messy head. "Is this beef jerky in your hair?"

"It's been a very rough two days." *Put your hands on me. Tell me you love me. Make this right.* "But if there had been no more planes, no more demonic rental vans, and no buses, I would've ran here. I came back to tell you that *you*, Noah Kincaid, are what I want."

His piercing eyes held hers, and Emma thought the earth had time to spin a full rotation before Noah finally spoke.

"Emma?" His voice, hoarse and raw.

"Yes?"

"I love you."

Emma threw herself into Noah's arms. "Thank, God." And she kissed her love with all the certainty she needed. Right there in his arms was where she belonged. She had finally found her place. It wasn't glamorous, it didn't come with a VIP press pass, and nobody would ever greet her every morning to do makeup and hair. But pressed next to Noah's beating heart, his strong hands holding her tight, it was an extravagance no TV show could ever offer.

She trailed kisses along Noah's sandpaper cheek, as she dug into his pocket, pulled out his phone, and peeked at the time and smiled. 11:59 p.m. She'd gotten her man for Christmas with one minute to spare. "This is the best Christmas ever." He was her present. No bow required.

"I saw you on TV." His lips lingered at her temple.

The mention still made her stomach wobble. "I had every intention of picking up where I'd left off." She wrapped her arms about Noah's waist and looked into his eyes. "But thirty minutes in, and I couldn't do it. I was miserable without you, and I knew that feeling wasn't going to go away. I didn't want to end up like my dad. I don't want his version of love. I want a life that brings me joy, that fills me up. A life without you could never make me happy."

"Em, if you want to work in New York, I'll go."

"Pretty sure I'm not welcome in that town. And I don't want to be there. This is where I'm meant to be."

"Are you absolutely sure? I don't want you to regret what you're giving up."

"I've only given up the things I should have a long time ago. I just couldn't see it. I'm all in."

Noah lifted her chin with his thumb and brushed his lips over hers.

"But"—she pressed her hand to his chest and took a small step back—"I need you to be all in, too. Because I'm not good at this relationship stuff. The very words *roots* and *permanence* make me itchy with hives." Emma wanted her voice to sound daring and certain. But the hesitancy came through anyway. "So maybe we don't put down roots. Maybe we put down love and memories. And children and laughter."

Noah took her hand and sealed her palm with his lips. "I like this idea."

Who needed an energy drink when relief was the ultimate high? "Oh, I'm full of ideas. This is why I'm a great marketing director. That job is still open, right?"

"Nah." Noah winked. "I gave it to Delores."

"I guess I'll have to wrestle it back from her."

"I think I might like to see that."

"Noah?" Emma leaned up and kissed his skin. "Would you marry me?"

His entire body ceased to move. "That's my question."

"I'm full of bold declarations lately."

He slid a piece of her wayward hair through his fingers. "This one's mine." Then the most gorgeous, most beautiful man in all of Sugar Creek eased down to one knee right beside the manger. The very place Emma had dropped her new Christmas prayer. "Emma Sylvia Sutton . . ." He clasped her hand in his. "Will you marry me?"

"Yes. Oh, my word, yes." Emma didn't even give him time to stand. She dropped to the ground and pulled her fiancé to her. She kissed him with all the love and hope that bubbled within her like the fountain on the square. "I'm probably going to drive you crazy, Noah Kincaid."

He pressed his forehead to hers. "I'm counting on it."

"Merry Christmas, Noah." In her hands, Emma held the face of the greatest love she had known. "You are the best gift I could ever receive."

"Merry Christmas, Emma."

Beneath the Star of Bethlehem, Emma promised her heart to the boy she had fallen for so many years ago. The Wise Men still held their gifts. Joseph still bowed in prayer. Mary looked on and smiled, this woman-child who had just given the world the good news they'd been waiting for.

The Christ child was born. The silence had ended.

And somewhere beneath that wide-eyed, puffy-haired doll in the manger sat Emma's prayer.

More than a crumbled bit of paper, it was hope piercing the fear.

Because on this night, Emma Sutton had finally found her Christmas.

TURN the page for a preview of *His Mistletoe Miracle,* book two in the series.

HIS MISTLETOE MIRACLE PREVIEW

He needs a fake girlfriend. She needs a holiday miracle.

After years as a hostage in Afghanistan, wounded journalist Will Sinclair retreats to idyllic Sugar Creek, Arkansas, to finish his memoir and get his life back on track. As if the town's match-making mamas aren't enough trouble, his own meddling family descends on him for the holidays. To get them all off his back, Will plots a ridiculous idea. He just needs the right woman. When he finds a bossy decorator in his yard, it's more than her ugly Christmas sweater that makes her the perfect pick.

Cordelia Daring loves her life as a foster mom and entrepreneur. But when she finds herself in need of money, Will's offer comes just in time. Pretend to be his girlfriend for two weeks? She can handle that. Sure, she flunked drama in high school, but how hard could it be to pose as the arm candy of famous journalist Will Sinclair? Never mind that her foster son adores him. Or that his family is everything she's ever wanted. Because when the deal expires, Cordelia intends to take her money and run.

As the holiday draws near, their pretend relationship spirals out of control. And Cordelia's not sure she wants it to unravel. If these two hope to make it till December 25th, they're going to need some serious Christmas magic. .

CHAPTER 1

A Sinclair man knew how to charm a woman. It was in his smile. In his slow Southern lilt. In his obnoxiously beautiful DNA.

Will Sinclair was no exception.

But the former network reporter no longer had the clean-cut pretty boy face. His wavy blond hair had mysteriously darkened in captivity and was now longer than necessary, falling over his shirt collar. If you looked close enough, you might find a fleck or two of gray. Not that he cared. His face needed the attentions of a sharp razor and shaving cream. Four years in captivity changed a man. It could break you. At the very least, alter the heart.

But did it keep the ladies of Sugar Creek away?

No, it did not.

That was true today more than ever. He'd had a bad night of poker, too little sleep, and one soon-to-be former friend to thank for all of it.

Will had survived torture and imprisonment, but as his doorbell rang for the third time, he didn't know if he would survive this small Arkansas town. He stomped to the foyer, certain it would be someone of the female persuasion.

Will had barely finished his long-suffering sigh by the time he peeled open the door. "Good morning, Mrs. Beasley," he said to the woman smiling at his appearance. "You are a vision in that muumuu."

Shivering against the blistering December wind, the plump widow stood beside a porch post whose paint job had long expired. "My dear, I just stopped by to invite you to Christmas dinner. And to give you a taste of my cooking, I brought this coconut cream pie." She waved the baked good so close to his face, he nearly got a nose full of meringue. "Homemade crust."

Pie could make any man cave into temptation. "I bet this is your Blue Ribbon recipe, isn't it?" She blushed under his praise. "I'll just put it with . . . the rest."

"Do you know who else loves my pie?"

He didn't need a GPS to know where this was headed.

"My Alisha." Mrs. Beasley winked a brown eye. "You probably remember her from your childhood summers in Sugar Creek. She's all grown up now." She patted his bicep and gave an appreciative murmur. "Just like you."

"You tell her I said hello. And thank you for thinking of me. That's sure thoughtful of you. Now, if you'll excuse me, I have work—"

"Alisha would love to see you again. She moved back a few months ago." The gray-headed woman lowered her voice. "Nasty divorce. But not a bit of it was her fault."

"I'm sure it wasn't."

"We'd love to see you at our table. Give you two kids a chance to catch up on old times."

"I'm swamped with work, but thank you for the invitation." He'd been staring at the same chapter on his manuscript for days, but surely that still qualified as achievement. "So nice of you."

Peace and quiet. That's all Will wanted. He'd been here three months, and word had finally gotten out, despite his low profile. And regardless what his interfering family in South Carolina thought, he wasn't living like a mole. He'd shown his face in town maybe two or three times. Hung out at the diner with Noah, the town's mayor and his childhood friend. He was about to overdose on talking and civilities. Because, as he'd feared, the good folks of Sugar Creek now knew he was living there. And they were bent on smothering him with howdy-dos and casseroles.

"Thanks again, ma'am," Will said.

"I'll set a place for you at the table! And if you happen to hear of my Alisha coming off a gambling addiction, you do not pay that any mind."

"I know she's pure as an angel. Take care now."

And with that, he shut the door. Again.

After storing the pie in the refrigerator next to the banana pudding and a trifle, Will walked back down the hall to his office, a well-equipped and comfortable room in his vacation rental.

Wearing a gray Sugar Creek High School football t-shirt, dark jeans with his left knee peeking through, and no shoes, Will sat in his chair and propped his elbows on the burled walnut desk. Chapter seven was still just as blank as he'd left it when the doorbell rang the first time this morning. Just as blank as when he'd gone to bed last night. And just as blank as it had been this time last week.

He set his fingers to the keyboard. An old writing professor had once told him to just write, even if the words were nothing but junk. An empty page couldn't be edited.

Living as a hostage in the Middle East was a nightmare I

thought I'd never have to face as a reporter or world traveler. The risk was always there, but you don't think it could happen to—

The doorbell gonged again, and Will lowered his head to his keyboard. What now?

He descended the stairs again, rubbing an old wound, and wondered if he should just move the desk to the front door.

"Hello, Will." Rachel Sands stood on his porch in a red dress and black stilettos, a combination that promised things dark and beautiful. "I was just passing through."

It was two o'clock on a Wednesday. Didn't anyone have a job in this town?

"What can I help you with, Miss Rachel?" Will forced himself not to take a step back as Rachel moved in, leaning a hip against his door frame. If she were a cat, she'd be purring and rubbing against his ankles.

"Word around town is you don't have anywhere to go for Christmas dinner."

This was his fifth invite of the day, and Will knew exactly who to blame for this outpouring of hospitality. His mother and whomever her insiders were. Donna Sinclair might be at her home in Charleston, but she had a network of friends all over the globe, and she'd surely enlisted them like soldiers to look after her wayward son.

"I have plenty of places I could be," Will said. "I am not a man without a spiral ham."

She laughed prettily and shook her blonde hair, the highlighted color a contrast to the lengthy, black lashes she batted now. "We all know what you're gonna do." She slinked one step closer, her perfume a hammer to his already aching head. "You're gonna spend every day like the others—locked inside this house, working away."

"Now that's not entirely true." His years reporting the

news had never quite scrubbed his Southern drawl clean. "I'll also be watching sports and catching up on all the movies I've missed." Will attempted an amiable smile. "I do like to stay busy."

"I could help you with that."

In another life, he might've taken Rachel up on the offer. Now he felt tired even looking at her. "Your hospitality knows no bounds. You are too kind, Rachel." He glanced at his watch. "I'm sorry, I've got a conference call in five minutes. I need to—"

"Mayor Kincaid told me you needed some cheering up."

Ah, so that's who Will had to blame for today's parade of high-pressure sales.

Rachel clasped her hand on his. "My place. Seven o'clock, Christmas Eve." She gave his fingers a squeeze. "And I promise. . .dessert will be an indulgence you won't want to miss."

"I'll give that some thought. Now, I don't want to keep you. I know you have all that real estate to sell."

"Oh, I've always got time for—"

"Thanks for stopping by."

He shut the door right in her beauty pageant face and returned to his dusty office.

The worst part of captivity was the anger of surviving.

Somehow I had lived.

And twenty-three children had not.

The most brutal day of torture could not compare to the thoughts, the visions in my own head.

Another knock from downstairs interrupted the slow clack of Will's keyboard. He shot from his chair. "For the love of—"

Favoring that right leg, he marched to the foyer like a man with blood on his mind. He wrenched open the door.

"Look, sweetheart, if you're here to offer me a seat at your table for—"

"One night together, and we're already at the endearment stage?" Noah Kincaid took off his sunglasses and grinned.

"Get off my property, Mayor Kincaid." Will tried to shut the door, but Noah used his shoulder and nudged his way inside, bypassing Will and walking straight for the kitchen, as if he owned the place.

"Still a little sore about losing last night?" Noah reached into the stainless steel fridge and grabbed a water. "Your refrigerator's a disgrace. Do you eat anything besides peanut butter and hot dogs?"

"Yeah, a whole collection of desserts you're not welcome to. But after the day I've had, you really want to come in in here and disparage my Skippy?"

Noah's lips quirked, and he had the grace to look away.

"You got something to say?" Will asked.

"I say you need a freaking haircut and shave. You look like an intellectual grunge singer."

"This face got me three homemade pies by two o'clock. You know anything about that?"

"Doesn't sound familiar." Noah took a swig of water then smiled.

Will took a spoon to the center of the banana pudding. "Maybe if you can't handle losing a poker game, you shouldn't play."

"You cheated."

"How about you step closer and say that."

"You want to show me that deck of cards?"

"So to retaliate you tell every single girl and her mama that I'm desolate and alone for Christmas? This is the big bad revenge you said you were gonna get?"

"You say revenge." Noah sat down on the leather sofa with a piece of coconut cream pie. "I say it's just evidence of my caring heart. Plus, that's the price you pay for finally stepping out of your cave."

"You're gonna fix the mess you made, Noah" Will said. "I can't get a thing done with my door bell and phone ringing."

"You look like death," Noah said. "Your parents keep calling me wanting updates. They're worried sick."

"You know an upset family is the last thing I want, but I need some space."

"You should at least get out of the house more, so I can truthfully tell them you're not living like a hobbit."

"I did get out. And look where it got me—playing host to every single woman and her momma."

"Oh, the burden of being rich, famous, and an American hero."

Will's stomach burned with a familiar acid. He wasn't a hero. He was. . .Heck, he didn't know who he was anymore.

Noah picked at a piece of fuzz on the arm of the chair. "Will . . .sit down. I have some news I think you need to hear."

CHAPTER 2

Bam! Bam! Bam!

Will startled at the noise outside, all conversation forgotten. A guy didn't survive a bomb blast and not have the occasional kickback.

Rising anger fueled his steps as he strode to the living room window and cast a frustrated gaze to the scene. It looked like Santa's elves had escaped to his lawn.

"What's all that?" Noah asked as he joined him.

"No idea." There were people in his yard. Uninvited people.

And, from the looks of it, they had Christmas on their minds.

Flinging open the front door, a shoeless Will crossed the cold yard and approached a burly man toting a ladder. "What's going on?"

The guy jerked a thumb behind him. "I'm just the hired help. Talk to the boss."

Will turned and found a honey-haired woman standing in the middle of his yard with her back toward the road, a clipboard in one hand, a coffee cup in the other, and if he wasn't mistaken, a giant snowman protruding from her top knot.

"More lights, Cecil!" she shouted.

Oh, no. Will was not having this.

He stalked her like a lion after a gazelle and tapped her on the shoulder. "Excuse me."

She turned, a smile on her face and a baby attached to her hip by some mummy-like contraption. "Hello."

"Hi?" He nearly took a step back as her piercing gaze met his. With her olive skin, chestnut eyes, and pink cotton-candy smile, she was one beautiful interloper. Will reminded himself he needed to get back to work, and he couldn't tolerate one more interruption. "Hi is all you have to say? You're disturbing the neighborhood, you're trespassing on this property, and you and your *Bring Your Baby to Work Day* are desecrating my space with Christmas junk."

She tucked the clipboard under her arm and wrapped her free hand around the stocking-capped baby. "Christmas *junk*?"

Will pinched the bridge of his nose and prayed for patience. "What are you doing, ma'am?"

"My name is Cordelia." She offered her hand to shake. "Cordelia Daring of Daring Displays."

"Nice to meet you." At least she hadn't recognized him yet and gone all starry-eyed and requested a selfie or a potholder for her casserole. "I repeat, what are you doing?"

"Decorating."

He tried not to focus on the glittery decoration in her hair or her holiday sweater that flashed red and green in lighted intervals. "Why?"

Cordelia Daring's smile took on a less hospitable tilt. "I thought I'd start a trend by decorating for the holiday." She crossed her fingers. "Sure hope it catches on."

An impertinent trespasser at that. "I mean, why right now, right here?"

"Because I was feeding a baby and couldn't get here any earlier."

"Who authorized this?"

"The home owner."

On a tip from Noah, Will had leased the place online, having not so much as a phone call with the owner, Sylvie Sutton. Surely this was a rental violation of some sort. She couldn't dispatch a decorating crew to make his house look like the North Pole without at least a warning. "Can you just come back?"

"No," she said. "I can't." She jostled the baby and adjusted the cap over his ears to guard against the biting wind. "I have this crew for two hours and then—"

"Look, I'm trying to work," Will said.

"Oh, cool. Me too." Her brow lifted in a perfect arch of sarcasm. "So, how about you go back to your work, and I'll return to mine."

He dodged a man carrying an animatronic reindeer and bit back a curse. It was like he was stuck in a horrible made-for-TV Christmas movie. Where was the pause button? How did he change the channel?

"Miss Daring." Will softened his voice. As a former television journalist, he knew his husky timbre had defused many a sticky situation. "I'm here in Sugar Creek specifically for some peace and quiet."

"And you'll get it." That infuriating smile was back, dimpling her rosy cheeks and lighting her warm eyes. "As soon as the guys—"

"No, not in a few hours. I want quiet now." Forget tact and sexy TV voice. "You need to leave."

Hearing that, she drew herself up tall. "We can't. If I don't finish this job then I don't—"

"I'm sorry." He called out to the crew. "Time to go home, fellas. No Christmas for this house, but thank you anyway."

"You can't send them away."

"I just did."

"You don't own the property." She consulted that blasted clipboard. "Mrs. Sutton does, and I have her explicit instructions to, and I quote, 'Make that place look like Christmas is a plague that devoured the house.'"

"Oh, it's definitely sick."

"The decorating continues."

Will had once loved the holidays. He hadn't always needed an Epi-Pen for the anaphylactic shock of good tidings and tinsel. But he wanted nothing to do with it this year. After returning to the states, he'd gone back to his home in Atlanta. He'd ignored his parents' many requests to return to Charleston for Sinclair gatherings. Even when they'd mailed him a plane ticket, he simply stuck it in a drawer and left for Arkansas. Sugar Creek had been a vacation spot for his family growing up, but there was no longer anything quaint or relaxing about the town now. His old friend Noah should've warned him Sugar Creek had morphed into the South's leading tourist spot for small-town Christmas. It was nauseating.

The baby began to kick his legs and cry. "Shhh, it's okay, Isaiah. The grumpy man didn't mean to scare you with his loud voice and Scroogey ways."

Good heavens, now she was using the baby in her tactics. "You have five minutes to vacate the premises."

Cordelia pushed a gaudy star on her sweater, and it began to chime "Jingle Bells."

"I'm afraid you can't cancel Christmas," she said.

Will glared down at the psychotic elf. "You just watch me."

As if on cue his television movie took a horrible plot detour. A blue sedan crawled down the street, slowing as it neared his rent house, and a sick foreboding settled in the pit of Will's stomach. He didn't recognize that car, but it rolled toward them with an intention that he'd know anywhere. He saw the outline of hands wave from inside the vehicle as it confidently pulled into the driveway, the tires crunching over dead leaves and busted acorns.

"You've got to be kidding me." Will pressed two fingers to his throbbing temple as Cordelia's sweater changed tunes and the baby cried louder.

He'd been the recipient of a lot of visitors today. Each one more obnoxious than the next.

But these people arriving now?

They were next-level harassment.

A blight on his time and peace of mind.

Annoying wildflowers who showed up without invitation.

ABOUT THE AUTHOR

Get a free book from Jenny by signing up for her infrequent newsletter. www.jennybjones.com/news.

Award-winning author Jenny B. Jones writes romance, mystery, and YA with sass and Southern charm. Since she has very little free time, Jenny believes in spending her spare hours in meaningful, intellectual pursuits, such as checking celebrity gossip and pursuing her honorary PhD in queso. Jenny digs foster care, animal rescues, and her adorable son. She lives in the great state of Arkansas, where she's currently at work on her next novel and loves to hear from readers.

www.jennybjones.com

Insta: @jennybjonesauthor

Facebook: jennybjones

Twitter: JenBJones

ALSO BY JENNY B. JONES

MYSTERY, SWEET ROMANCE

Wild Heart Summer

A Katie Parker Production, Acts 4-6

Enchanted Events Mystery Series

His Mistletoe Miracle

A Sugar Creek Christmas

The Holiday Husband

Save the Date

Just Between You and Me

YOUNG ADULT

A Charmed Life series

In Between (Katie Parker, Book 1)

On the Loose (Katie Parker, Book 2)

The Big Picture (Katie Parker, Book 3)

Something to Believe In (Katie Parker, Book 4)

I'll Be Yours

There You'll Find Me

Made in the USA
Coppell, TX
17 December 2021